Advance Praise for
Triumph: Collected Stories

"Lizzie Harwood's beautifully written collection covers vast
landscapes, from France to New Zealand, from families
struggling to stay together to young women unable to find their
way, from the need to be heard to the dark desires of the human
heart. The array of moods, conflicts, and fears will keep readers
turning the pages. Lizzie Harwood is one of my favorite writers,
and this collection is a must for short story lovers."
Janet Skeslien Charles, author of *Moonlight in Odessa*

"Each story in *Triumph* draws you into its world immediately,
with compelling narrative and complex characters. Lizzie
Harwood has mastered the art of the short story—you'll feel as if
you've walked alongside the characters in their journeys... just in
time to move on to the next story." **Vicki Lesage, author of**
***Confessions of a Paris Party Girl* and**
Confessions of a Paris Potty Trainer

"Lizzie Harwood's writing sizzles with vivid language and
sensory descriptions, which linger in the reader's mind. The
stories are carefully wrought so as to reveal the complexity of
girls and women and their relationships to others. Human needs,
desires, and the underbelly of regret are thoroughly explored
with black humor. A highly engaging and original collection to
be read at once." **Elena Kaufman, writer and performer**

"You'll laugh, fear and wonder with these 'gone girls and
complicated women' who, in Lizzie Harwood's exuberant, electric
stories, manage to turn dismay into lusty self-derision, and
calamity into a reckless kind of strength." **Marie Houzelle,
author of *Tita* and *Belle-Famille***

"A fresh new expat riff on the secret life of girls—scandalous and
heartbreaking." **Laurel Zuckerman, author of *Sorbonne
Confidential* and *Les Rêves Barbares du Professeur Collie***

Triumph

Collected Stories

With an Introduction by
Jennifer Butler

Lizzie Harwood

Triumph: Collected Stories

ISBN: 10-digit: 2955069019
ISBN: 13-digit: 978-2-9550690-1-1

Edited by www.editordeluxe.com
Cover design by The Pixel Pusher: www.thepixelpusher.co.uk

Acknowledgment is made to the following, in which some stories in this collection first appeared: *Carve Magazine*: "Anon 1" as "Rome"; *The Best New Zealand Fiction, Volume 5* (Vintage, 2008): "Anon 2" as "Throat for Dinner"; and *Pharos*: "Lily" as "The Only Girl not For Sale."

Published by: Editor Deluxe Press

Dedication

To our amazing parents who defy gravity

Introduction by Jennifer Butler

An introduction. I want you to meet my husband, James. Or, I know someone with the same hobby, the same name, the same job, from the same school, the same doctor, the same country. You meet up. A new door opens. I introduce you to this collection of stories with the opening from "Anon 3," told from one of the various narrators all called "I." We have no idea what color eyes or how short or tall but we know her from the first paragraph.

I was twelve when we went to Toronto to our uncle's split-level house in Oakville. There were words that brought us to this: "sale of the house," "falling through," and "mortgage payments." I was in sharing with cousin Rowena, who drank rum and coke out of a plastic thermos she hid under her bed and sent me every midnight to make her French fries in their deep fryer.

Our narrator learns things about Rowena as the story unravels and in this unraveling there is a moment where we are with the narrator and she describes a lunchtime before she starts playing daily afternoon hooky from school: *I slunk around the library, taking a long time to eat my baloney sandwich then browsing books, pretending to belong, eventually sitting in a corner with something open I wasn't seeing.*

I choose this moment because it resonates with me, where a universal moment every "I" has issues forward. And Ms. Harwood finds a moment in each of these stories where the character is stuck, the stuff of which we make our own wings. Human beings are the only creatures who learn from the experiences of others and in these introductions we find solutions or comfort or humor even, friends.

Modern life. We have created this giant apparatus for some cultivation of hard skills while failing to develop the moral and emotional faculties down below. Who are we? We are our job. Children are coached on how to jump through scholastic hoops. By far, our most important decisions are about whom we will marry and whom to befriend, what to love and what to despise, and how to control impulses. We are good at talking about material incentives, but bad about talking about emotions and intuitions. We are good at teaching technical skills, but when it comes to the most important things like character, we have almost nothing to say.

The 10 narrators are an emotional and enchanted group. Their predicaments—girlie weekend getaways, broken promises, weddings, yoga retreats, homeless, jobless, feckless—highlight the importance of passions and per-ceptions. The author writes, with authority, about the power of relationships and the invisible bonds between people. The outer mind hungers for status and money and applause while this inner mind, Ms Harwood inhabits, is the hunger for harmony and connection—those moments when self-consciousness fades away and a person is lost in a challenge, a cause, the love of another or the love of God.

These characters, their unconscious maintains no distance from their environment but is immersed in it. They coat things with observant words. In "Stephanie," the narrator sits in a diner, wet jacket and annoyed, *Even before I sit down I know the waitress is useless because everyone stares at her to get her attention, rather than talking to each other.*

They have street smarts more than intellect. They know how to read people, situations and ideas. You can put them in front of a crowd, and they can develop a feel for the landscape— what can go together and what is never going to go together and what will never be fruitful. They react to human nature. In "Skye, Ingrid, Leo," the first narrator announces, *I turned seven without Mum—she went to Canada to see her Mum. I looked for Canada on the World Map Political at school—it was big and pink.* These small details which inform a character for her life. Small details to inform affections and aversions forever, individual experiences that are the stuff of real life.

There is a freshness about a group of stories set mostly in New Zealand where the names of beaches and towns and mountains are those I am hearing for the first time. Kaikoura.

Lost Jandal Creek. Rosalie Bay Road. Mulberry Grove. Shoal Bay. Rotorua. Blenheim. Mount Ruapehu. Fox Glacier.

Let me introduce you to this random page I just opened. Val, the operator of a small bed and breakfast, *She shows me a room upstairs. It screams floral, twin beds pushed together with a synthetic floral bedcover in blue and pink. Floral lampshades, floral wallpaper, thick green carpet with round floral rug. I press the bed; it jiggles.*

Here is the introduction. I'm certain you will get along.

Jennifer Butler

Paris, 2015

Young Women

Krista

LULU AND I ARE JETTING over to India for a girlie break!

I've had another spat with Harry, and Lulu was at a loose end with Antony away on work trips. Truth be told, it was more than a spat with Harry—he kicked me out. I daren't mention this to Lulu, she'd be heartbroken, she adores Harry. It's so sad when all your friends have to immediately despise the guy who's just broken your heart. Plus, she's married to Antony now and in all honesty I believe it's unkind to tell married friends of a break-up as it may affect their marriage adversely. I'd never want to upset Lulu. She is my best friend ever.

Harry's last words were a little harsh, he actually grabbed my arm as I made my dignified exit (after resisting the urge to set his suits on fire) and *shook my arm*. It was the first time he'd exhibited violence. His voice had a peculiar strain to it when he said, "You know, I don't know if I was ever in love with you, Krista. Not even for one second."

I can't repeat this kind of stuff to Lulu. She would bawl with total empathy. She tells me halfway across the Bay of Bengal that she thinks Harry's the kindest man alive and what a great couple we are and how she and Antony want us to come sailing with them in the Maldives this year. Lulu is an absolute pal, hand on heart I'd be a wreck without her—we met because Harry and Antony do business with each other. We're all in Singapore. (Though technically, I am, again, homeless. Harry-less. It's such rotten luck!)

I reply we'd love to come sailing. The sooner the better. We cheers to our holiday with the teeniest of vodka tonics, which tastes odd as the vodka's not even Smirnoff or Absolut, but 'Muscovy' made in Bangalore. Too funny!

We shun luxury. Luxury is for weekends away with Antony and Harry—for our girlie break it is three-star hotels maximum, and we are ruthlessly fixed on spending half the time in an ashram. Lulu knows all about such places.

"They teach tantric sex tricks," she says during the taxi trip to the hotel. Our taxi is driven by an absolutely teddy bear called Babu.

"Of course, I'll have to tell Harry we're going for the yoga." But in my heart of hearts, I figure I can do with some new tricks. Singapore is not the kind of place to hang out in unless you have a sponsor, I won't last long alone there, despite the money Harry threw at me before he changed the locks. Lulu says that being married, one immediately realizes one needs new tricks, too.

We're spoiled for choice on hotels and luck upon Abu the Reception Manager at the Hotel Marina Palace, who ushers us into a Deluxe Twin with A/C for 600 a night—since it's low season and he says we are such beautiful strangers to India. I have a feeling I am about to meet my soul mate here in Kovalam! The lighthouse at the end of the beach is my sign. And this is bloody India, for Christ's sake. It's all about enlightenment, spiritual bliss, and Ayurvedic treatments. We shimmy down the beach, with the shop boys hanging out of their shacks calling, "Hello, Stranger!" and "I'm waiting for you, Darling!"

I explain to Lulu that Harry absolutely requires me to buy a stunning necklace for myself: this is my mission for the trip. Something that looks like a string of candy, he said. He's so cute and American like that. Lulu is happy to have something to do, I'm sure, although she vaguely mentioned a yen to draft a new book here while lying on the beach. She's written a few children's books. I don't even know why she still 'works' with the wicket Antony's on and anyway dreaming up stories about bears lost in the woods, or whatever, is something I'm sure anyone could do. But I'd never mock Lulu's chosen field, not even in the privacy of my own thoughts. She is my top friend, after all. I ooze total support.

My initial *coup de foudre* with Kovalam and the Hotel Marine Parade packs up overnight when invisible things in my mattress eat me alive. By daybreak I'm an ill-at-ease, puffy, miserable girl; even my eyelids have ballooned! I ring Abu who sends citronella up with condensed milk coffees. Small consolation—I am hideousness personified! This will really devastate my chances of finding any sort of soul mate on the beach today.

Lulu's mattress is safe from the bedbugs. I realize being Harry-less goes deeper than having no penthouse apartment with panoramic view to call home. I am fated to suffer more than safe, married Lulu. Antony protects her even long distance. When he rings her, I pretend to ring Harry and laugh and laugh out on the balcony so Lulu's day won't be destroyed by my sad news.

"Harry says hiya!" I grin.

"Antony said he saw him last night down at the yacht club, he had quite a few in him and was in a foul mood."

Lulu has an unattractive crease in her forehead.

"Poor Harry, a deal went south with Seoul. Too harsh!"

"Hhhm," says Lulu.

I am all on my own. Battling unseen forces.

Abu, my utter savior, promises to change my mattress today while we are out.

On the beach, we politely decline beach mats from hawkers with Cockney accents who append every entreaty with "beautiful darling." We also turn down mangos from the cheery fruit-selling women, whose mouths are stained red with betel nut, who twirl machete knives awfully close to our bikini tops. But the ladies only step away when Lulu says "No, thank you." Me, I end up getting my palm read by a wizened crackpot in a turban with no teeth and only a ratty loincloth for clothing. Then the pot-bellied lifeguards bark at me for overpaying.

"But he predicted I'd be married next year!" I protest to deaf ears.

It seems I've caused a bull market by paying the palm-reader one hundred rupees. Now everyone wants a piece of the pie and the locals converge on the pigeon-chested man, who trembles in fear. The lifeguards converge to break up the crowd and we clear out to one of the many cafes, wall-to-wall with German tourists, and order *upma*, cheese toasties, and a mild dhal curry for brunch. Lulu says she'll never get any work done on the beach at this rate.

Only after the third night does Abu find me a mattress that isn't teeming. Our mission to find my necklace has led us in and out of each and every one of the dozens of shacks selling jewelry strewn along the beachfront. We examine strings of sunstone, loops of tiger eye, chokers of aventurine, turquoise, malachite, amber, rose quartz, amethyst, jade, all weighty and smooth under our fingertips like giant lollipops. As the four o'clock monsoon hits we take cover in one shack near the hotel where two skinny guys, Ging and Shamim sit against the walls playing a card game called Shithead. Ging tells us they are from Kashmir so have the best necklaces, they are the only Muslim shop owners in Kovalam and his family wants him to marry a good girl very soon. Two minutes later he tells me he is crazy in love with me and proposes. What do you know, that palm-reader may have been right! But I tell Ging straight off I'm with the love of my life already and as consolation we buy postcards from their array of washed-out lighthouse images.

Back in the hotel we watch the remake of *Sabrina* with Julia Roberts as the Audrey Hepburn character, drinking condensed milk coffees, smoking and scribbling platitudes on the postcards, which we send via Abu (mine to Harry, of course, and Lulu's to Antony and her parents back in Sydney). It's too mad—Lulu and I are both Double Bay born and bred, (although she didn't get sent off to boarding school for "wayward girls") and we were at university the same year (I had to drop out—too dull), but we never met there. You wouldn't read about it! Lulu's asked me who I was friends with in Sydney but I can't even remember. It was a billion lifetimes ago. But cross my heart and hope to die, I'll never go back. That Sydney scene is just too—stifling. I could never breathe there.

What I mean is, people meet people but there's always someone who knows someone who knows you so they think they know you before even meeting and somehow I had a reputation (which wasn't me at all) when I left there eons ago. I'm a gone girl and proud of it. Singapore is me. To a tee. Although, Singapore has become old hat of late, always *sama-sama* at the yacht club especially with all the nicest, most entrepreneurial expat guys jumping ship to mainland China. Maybe Shanghai is me.

The next day I cave and buy Ging's blindingest necklace— a mixed bag of color with stones the size of jawbreakers. I look like a queen in it. It costs nine hundred rupees. Ging gives it to me for four hundred if we promise to come to their place for dinner that night. Why not! An invite to eat local— how sweet!

At sundown we meet Ging and Shamim at the shop and they walk us over the hill to their place on a pitch-black track along with other locals who work down on the beach. I recognize a few of the fruit-selling ladies but they don't smile. Inside the boys' quaint concrete bungalow, strip lighting illuminates one large room with the kitchen to the side (no fridge, rudimentary hob, rigged up tap) they have one hassock couch, a TV with bunny ears for antennae, mats on the floor. A banquet of Kashmiri curries is presented in gold metal dishes, lots of lamb, hotter and darker than the Kerala vegetarian offerings and we drink the port we brought, which is our biggest mistake: fuelled by booze the lads transmogrify into tragic, obsessive, insistent wooers (by now Shamim is in love with Lulu and being in love with a married woman "make him crazy"). We are coaxed up a ladder to the rooftop to watch the stars and Ging is in my ear so much about marriage that I stand suddenly, go to the edge of the rooftop and say, "Enough. This is a sham. You don't really love us; you don't even know what love is. Take us back to the hotel this second."

They fall silent and lead us down the dark path, saying goodnight sulkily. In our room we watch *So I Married an Axe Murderer* but Lulu's in an odd mood.

"You certainly let rip on the roof."

"What do you mean?"

"You were so… angry. They were harmless."

"They ticked me off."

"How are things with Harry? Everything fine?"

"Absolutely. He is a doll. We're blissfully happy. Truth is, I think he's on the verge of proposing."

"Hhhhm."

That crease is back above her eyes.

We up camp and head for the ashram. It's two hours' drive away at some dam. Abu promises to keep our room now that I have a mattress that's not hopping. We leap into our

Ambassador taxi with our favorite chauffeur, Babu2. Are these their real names, I wonder, or the names they give us to say?

On the way up the final hill we pass backpackers who are literally *walking* here. Too crazy, in this heat! It's a thousand times hotter inland than on the coast. Babu2 lets us out at the bottom of a crumbly flight of stone stairs. At reception, a Japanese woman with her hair bound into Princess Leia buns hands us the list of rules and some waiver to sign in case of death. She doesn't speak. The list is all CAPS LOCKED on recycled paper:

NO ANIMAL PRODUCT, NO CIGARETTE, NO ALCOHOL, NO NARCOTIC, NO COFFEE, NO BAD CLOTHE, NO NON-SPIRITUAL READING MATERIAL, NO INCENSE (didn't India invent the stuff?), NO FOOD BURIED IN THE EARTH (that one throws us, but Princess Leia clarifies in the highest-pitched, whispery falsetto I've ever heard: "No onion, no garlic, no food come up." The woman has the blank look of wall-mounted game fish.) NO MOBILE PHONE, COMPULSORY ATTENDANCE FOR ALL ACTIVITY (there's a list from 5.30am) MEDITATION, HATHA YOGA, LECTURE, MEAL, KARMIC YOGA (is this the code for Tantric Sex?), HATHA YOGA, FREE TIME, DINNER, MEDITATION & CHANTING. LIGHT OUT 10.30PM.

Princess Leia points to the waiver. "You sign *here*. You put next-of-kin *here*."

For next-of-kin I write Harry, noting that Lulu peeks to see who I put.

Princess tells us there is no refund if we leave early. Even her voice sounds like it has been tracked down and shot. It's 300 rupee a night in our own cabin. 180 if we share in the dorm. We go for our own cabin so at least we'll be able to laugh hysterically at how mad this place is!

We follow Princess down a stone path past a shop where she jabs at ugly pajama tee shirts and pants until we realize our shorts and tank tops are unacceptable attire. The cotton drawstring pants are dyed a weak lilac, smell like dust, and would fall to bits in any normal wash cycle.

I grow brave following the swaying buns further down the path. "How long have you been here?"

Princess Leia pauses and does a funny pirouette mid-path.

"Six months. It is bliss. I don't remember Japan."

That's when I know we are in a cult. Lulu looks at me. Her eyes widen; I squint in reply. We pass a beaming stocky blonde who waves, "*Namaste!*"

Princess whispers in awe, "Uta is here *one year.*" Clearly this is Princess's goal if she still has a concept of the Gregorian calendar in another six months' time.

"Which guru leads here?" Lulu reads widely, she knows words like 'guru' and 'swami': the lingo of the enlightened.

"We have Swami Rick. He is amazing." Princess shivers with rapture and she smiles, showing anemic gums.

"He's American?" Lulu says.

Princess hardly blinks. "He's under the Guru Hajidhaba."

Lulu has nothing to add.

It takes Princess ten minutes to unlock the door to our miniscule cabin. She is so dopey her fistful of keys all fail to work and she is obliged to meander back to the office for the correct set. These people are not operating on all cylinders.

Inside I say, "Let's blow this popsicle."

"We paid for two nights. Let's give it 24 hours. The yoga could be great."

"Okay then." I pick at my pearly pinky-silver nail polish and resist the urge to gnaw at a hangnail. Who knows what viral infection lurks under my nails by now? It's one-thirty. Too late for lunch. We've missed out on the Karmic Yoga (our dwindling hope of tantric sex classes). Just in time for the two-hour stint of afternoon yoga.

We put on our pajama pants and tee shirts to cover our shoulders and I pretend to surreptitiously text Harry while Lulu surreptitiously texts Antony before we turn off our phones and hide them under the canvas sacking they call a mattress here. A plume of dust ascends when the mattresses drop.

Yoga is a grueling affair presided over by a pot-bellied baldy in a badly draped toga droning on about breathing. The mats smell of a thousand unwashed strangers. We stand on our heads for so long I can't help but notice the man opposite me. He is tall, taller than Harry, with cropped brown hair, virile shoulders, ice blue eyes and a face that's turning beetroot. Hello stranger, beautiful darling!

Everyone takes a cup of chai afterwards. They swarm the sugar bowl, heaping lumps into their teacups like there's no tomorrow. The cracked porcelain bowl is clearly the only source of sucrose in this joint. The group consists of flabby English girls and grubby European men with bad teeth and body odor, along with the compulsory Antipodeans scattered like lost sheep. Except for Beautiful Stranger, who doesn't need his chai sweetened, standing on his own across the wall-less pagoda. I go over and introduce myself. He says he's from Israel. He has good teeth.

"What brings you here?"

"I come for break from Army. I drive tank."

"Really?"

"I study computer but then I have military service but I am too good and I become Tank Commander. I have nine tank. Now they want me do Army for all my life. So I take one-year break. My father, businessman. I am only child. Tel Aviv is very nice, very pretty. But for me, there will be only tank."

I murmur, "I see…" He's so open, unmanipulative, so unlike Harry with his starched shirt formalities and unwillingness to talk about how much money his family has or how the inheritance will be parceled out. I am drawn to this man's bicep pulsing under his thin cotton shirt. He smells like citronella. I wonder how old his parents are; they could knock off sooner rather than later. I don't even know his name, but I can see myself carrying his babies. Asia is so late '90s, the Middle East would be far more *me*. Tel Aviv is bound to have some charming pockets… suddenly I am giddy and breathless with pure, spiritual (but physical also) *love* for this utter stranger. I look into his icy blue eyes and see my future.

Dinner is tasteless vegetal gunk on a metal tray and the turmeric turns my nail polish bile yellow because we eat with our fingers. Right-handed. Sitting on the floor. I am back in kindergarten here. Nobody speaks apart from some god-awful chanted blessing for the muck we are eating. Children are glimpsed. Definitely not a tantric sex hotspot. Definite cult vibe from the vacant smiles. Tank Commander comes to sit beside me along with a string of jolly, annoying girls from Essex. Tank Commander has a name: Dov. I kind of preferred calling him Tank Commander. He pronounces my name beautifully: K*rrrrr*ista. Krista with the *rrrr* all exotic and Middle Eastern-like. Lulu's eyebrows rise when he cracks a joke and I laugh.

Next is Meditation and Chanting down by the water—a haven for mosquitoes. I start itching from the get-go. Dov chants like a pro. Finally we see the head honcho, Swami Rick—who is disappointingly American-looking, with shaved head, draped in orange, and a nasal whine exactly like Doctor Evil in the *Austin Powers* movies. Too side-splitting! He sits cross-legged so we all have to endure his lack of underwear as he indoctrinates us: "*Now, Group, what is wrong with the Outside world?*" Nobody answers. "*Corruption. Low Moral Fiber. People who Flit from Thing to Thing. People who use People.*" I can't keep a straight face. I fidget when we're supposed to be meditating. I want to sneak off, but Dov is behind me and I want him to think I'm noble, a strong Amazon woman, oozing moral fiber. Mosquitoes form a cloud around my head like a halo.

We go to the pagoda for a chai and everyone's buzzing out from their sugar lumps and some Canadian dude plays guitar badly, and people talk about how malaria pills actually give you malaria and liver damage. Wake up, people! Lulu gives me dirty looks, but I ignore her. Dov and I laugh and chat and drink chai and the stars are very bright.

Around ten o'clock everyone yawns and says goodnight and it's a ghost town within five minutes. Dov walks Lulu and I to our cabin and I want to invite him in, but having Lulu around is such a handbrake.

I say, "Good night then…" and he gives me this intense stare and touches my hand. I am pure bliss. It is happening, folks, my soul has found its true mate.

Inside, Lulu starts up: "What the hell are you doing, Krista? You're with Harry!"

"What? I'm not doing anything!"

I can't even go outside for a cigarette and some peace and quiet because the Lights-Off Patrol are doing the tour, making sure everyone's tucked up in bed and not out having orgies. I'll bet Swami Rick is getting a blowjob from Princess Leia right this minute. I huff and puff and can't sleep and Lulu says, "We should leave tomorrow."

"Absolutely," I say. I try to think how to suggest that we stay a little longer.

Morning meditation is even worse—the mosquitoes bite inside my ears, in every nook and cranny they can find. Swami Rick drones on, *"Achieve your Higher Vibration. Your Higher Groove. Set your Body and Mind Free."* I want to set his toga on fire. Dov sits between Lulu and I. After the two-hour mozzie gorge, I tell him we are making our escape. His blue eyes cloud over and I look down, painting wistful regret all over my face, then back up straight into his eyes and tell him how beautiful it is down in Kovalam.

"We could do yoga on the beach. Eat mangos. Drink *coffee*."

Dov seems confused. Perhaps he likes it here. He's been chanting with enthusiasm, after all. I walk back up to the cabin by myself, leaving him down by the water to think it over: Krista or Malnutrition in a Cult? I glance back to make sure he is watching me walk up the hill. He is.

At the top of the hill, I bump into Swami Rick, who's so dopey, he walks like a geriatric although close up I can see he's no older than forty. Which is still ancient.

"Peace, sister," he says.

"Sure."

"Wait."

"What?"

"You are not at peace. Come."

He leads me by the wrist to a bench along the path, like I'm a child needing a time out.

"I just endured two hours of your indoctrinating bull crap, being bitten alive..."

"Sssssssssh. Breathe. From here."

He puts his hand on my belly. Too pervy!! I am about to scream 'Molestation!' when I see Dov mount the crest of the hill, so I tip my head back in a spiritual-ecstasy pose, screw shut my eyes, and breathe down to the depths of my belly.

If this doesn't float Dov's boat, nothing will.

Colors explode behind my eyelids and the light touch of Swami Rick's hand on my belly suddenly expands to a throbbing elephantine mitt that pulsates and seems to reach inside me to massage my heart, lungs, organs, right down to my solar plexus, and the ringing heavens open the doors, and

I float through into a nirvana of flowers blossoming and denuding, and every cell in my body is singing in a million-part harmony one incredible, beautiful, ringing sound of bliss.

"Peace."

Swami Rick removes his hand from my belly. The symphony and nirvana shut up shop and I open my eyes to see his greasy bald head bowed in thought and Dov motionless on the path staring at me like I am the way and the light. I grab Swami Rick's hand and press it to my lips.

"Thank you, that was...."

"Peace. Even for one second, it is more than enough."

"That's so true! Just one second of that is everything."

Swami Rick leaves.

Dov approaches, biting his lip with envy, "He never speaks directly, maybe after months, but never first day."

In our cabin, Lulu's on her forbidden cell phone, arranging with Abu for Babu2 to spirit us out of here by one o'clock.

"I can't leave! Swami Rick has just shown me heaven!"

"You're sick, Krista. Sure the people here are whacked. But they're experiencing something they're into. You don't have to keep saying Swami Rick's running an orgy out back."

"I'm serious. I'm staying here. Harry kicked me out."

Lulu doesn't look surprised. Antony must have told her.

"So you broke up even before this trip?"

"He's been really awful to me recently. He's really a bastard—he practically beat me up, one time..."

This isn't true, but I'm sick of Lulu's knowing look and she's such a well-brought up girl that she and Antony would never ask Harry if that was true or not.

"So Dov's your new sugar daddy? You've been flirting like mad since he mentioned his father owns five properties."

"Dov is a sweetie but I wouldn't call him my soul mate..."

"Who is now? That indoctrinating sham? Last night was non-stop jokes and sarcasm about him being Doctor Evil's twin and now you're suddenly enlightened?"

"You wouldn't understand."

"You just move from person to person, don't you?" Lulu is shouting now. "You're like a leech, sucking everything out of everyone you attach yourself to! We were never really friends, were we, Krista? Not even for one second."

"One second is enough. It is bliss."

"You've cracked."

That's when I know Lulu and I are not going to remain friends. But that's okay.

She doesn't go to morning Yoga or the Lecture and leaves before Karmic Yoga. The group stares in shock as she walks down the crumbly stone steps in her revealing skirt and singlet, cigarette ready on her lips to light up. Dov stands beside me, but already I feel a chasm between us, he tries so hard to meditate and chant right, but I can sense he hasn't ever reached the vibration I reached today and Swami Rick is never going to give him the time of day. But he is a sweetheart; he bought the necklace off me for his mother so I can afford to stay here longer. I told him it cost 1,800 rupees.

"Say bye to Ging and Shamim!" I call out.

Lulu gives me the finger through the back window of Babu2's Ambassador.

Dov gives me a hug; I'm so distraught about Lulu. He suggests we do Karmic Yoga together, which I quickly twig is cleaning toilets with soap that doesn't lather. I let him handle the bulk of it, fixing my sights on Swami Rick's private hut in the midst of the enclosure.

After the toilet scrub down it's Free Time. Dov heads into the nearby town to post the necklace to his mother. I go knock on Swami Rick's door. I wait for it to open. I could tell from his eyes. He's been waiting for the right girl to pass through here who truly understands. A girl like me.

Lily

WHEN LILY WAS TWENTY, she went to Amsterdam. On August 29th she was supposed to meet Mike at the Bulldog Cafe in the red light district. At three p.m. It was written on a piece of paper. She was in the heroin-dealers' district in the attic of Thomas—a friend of her sister's ex-boyfriend. Lily and Mike planned on traveling round together for a few weeks. Berlin, Paris, Rome, Budapest, Vienna, maybe Transylvania, maybe Greece. Nobody had email, not in 1993. It was the Bulldog Café or the abyss. Lily was there at five to three—she scoured the place, but no Mike. The waitress shook her head, "But there's seven Bulldogs—four in the red light district!" Lily got directions and went from Bulldog to Bulldog, through an increasing funk of dope smoke and hunger. She hadn't eaten except for that big latte and a slice of dark Dutch bread with marmalade. She felt a bit stoned and her vision grew hazy. At the last Bulldog, Lily looked through the picture window and Mike sat there—stoned with a halo of smoke around his head.

"I knew if I just sat tight you'd find me," he grinned, holding a joint out to her. His hair curled past his shoulders and he wore a white cotton shirt and beige cargo pants.

Mike came back to meet Thomas, the friend of Lily's

sister's ex-boyfriend, who immediately got them very stoned and cooked pasta and took photos of them laughing on his double bed watching MTV. Thomas was forty-three and a Sagittarian. Lily and Mike were youth, were so cute on the bed.

"You know what," Thomas snapped another photo. "You two should have sex together."

Lily laughed and then Mike joined in. "No, no," they hooted. "We're just friends."

They went out walking and Thomas led them through thin alleys with girls in every picture window and Lily was the only girl not for sale. Thomas brought up the sex thing all week—every time Lily and Mike rolled in from another museum up his wonky attic stairs, stoned off their faces—he claimed it would be a beautiful union, a communion of their souls. That they were made for each other. Yin and yang. "No, no," they repeated. Lily didn't want to mess up the travel plans, Mike had his ex-girlfriend back home he still hoped to marry. But with the untold dope, Mike may have felt vulnerable. Thomas kept needling. Lily kept climbing the tiny crooked stairs to the attic bed alone, leaving Mike to discuss the world with Thomas until the early hours. She lay awake listening to their voices.

It was their last night. Tomorrow would be Berlin. Last night to get stoned and to laugh. Mike cracked and went out, "I'm going to see a prostitute," he said. He returned after an hour with an aura around him that Thomas said was golden.

"She was so pretty. Wore white underwear, you know, I looked in all the picture windows and she looked the nicest.

Vietnamese. Beautiful girl. Beautiful. She made it something beautiful."

Thomas clapped his hands with glee. Lily didn't know what to feel when Mike went into details. She turned her head to watch MTV. But she listened to every word Mike said.

Anon 1

I AM NOT EVEN a nanny, I am some experiment.

I'm supposed to talk to the Albaneses in English. It's a lousy business when the children go off to school and the mother dresses up in her fur and traipses off with her mother, in her fur, like two Mummy bears, off to the fruit market in Piazza San Lorenzo to select lettuce leaves. I have a lot of free time until I have to pick up the children with the driver, who looks like Clint Eastwood and carries a gun, in case the children are kidnapped.

My middle day consists of streets and buses.

I take the orange bus over to Piazza di Spagna and sit on the steps, the Spanish ones, and stare into thin air. Thin winter air. I catch the scent of mandarins and then my mind automatically adds the smell of Body Shop Dewberry perfume and instead of thin air, all I can see is a room on floor nine and hear my sister talk about being on a Japanese tanker—the room goes up and down as if she's at sea—because she's on morphine. Apples and mandarins sit in a bowl nearby, along with wilting, decaying flowers, helium balloons and cards and cards and cards. There's a smell of Dewberry perfume because we sprayed on my sister's matted hair, to encourage familiar scents and bring her out of her coma. Her long hair grew so matted we had to cut it all off. The wooden drawers soon were choked full of her things we'd bring from her flat to the hospital, on the number seven red bus that passed through Seven Dials. My bus.

Today the piazza is quiet. It is a Wednesday. But I am not a nanny, I'm not legitimately able to hang out in Piazza Navona with a pushchair full of something kicking and crying in perfect Italian, and make friends with the other nannies. I have no pushchair, I can't hang out here. If I try to edge in, slink past or say *buon giorno*, then I get funny looks. So I walk back from Piazza di Spagna, or walk there and bus back. Or bus there and back. Any variation works out the same. I eat Baci Kisses all the way there and all the way back. Inside each silver-skinned chocolate are messages about love in four languages that I read to myself to improve my Italian. I phone home from the orange telephones with a calling card. I look in shop windows and wonder why every passing stranger wears that same shade of chocolate brown. I see Burberry every single day. I stand at a bar and drink macchiato.

The orange bus is crowded with leering men and I often feel a hard-on press against me. They pretend it's because the bus is too full. I never yell at them though, I always slink off the bus at the first available stop like I'm to blame. My number seven red bus in Brighton was never like that.

My mother stayed and I stayed to be there for my sister, but then Mom had to fly back home, so I stayed the longest. This became even longer in my recollection of the time. It became my struggle, alone, with nobody to talk to, my burden, a few incredibly lonely months. I was left holding the can. The can contained a broken sister, run down on a Tuesday afternoon by a white Peugeot 207, by an eighteen-year-old idiot, only four years younger than her, only two years younger than me and yet so stupid that he broke her skull and ruptured internal organs with his windshield and then dragged her fifty yards down the road, dragged her by her arm and broke that and after the fifty yards of dragging—when he finally remembered which pedal was the brake, he ran over both her legs, breaking them in four places each. Then he stopped the car.

I am careful crossing the roads in Rome, when I get off the bus with the leering men and continue my journey by foot. I sometimes walk in the other direction, to the Vatican, to San Pietro and stand in the vast circular space and stare up at the windows where sometimes the pope appears, tiny with a red rug hanging out his window to advertise his holy presence. I am supposed to be talking to Signora Albanese, the mother, to improve her English, but she's dressed up in her furs again, and waddles in her thin stockings and brown heels, off with her mother to select the lettuce leaves. This puts me at a loss. Today I come to the Vatican, tomorrow the Spanish Steps. I can't seem to find any other place to go explore in the whole city of Rome. Everything's limited by my mind.

The hours were full in Brighton all summer. No chance even for a break. I drank many cups of tea with powdered milk, out of polystyrene cups. And I ate scones with small desiccated raisins; processed scones that formed a ball of dough on the roof of your mouth as you chewed them up. And Galaxy chocolate bars. I didn't drink or smoke. I had to have something. When Mom was still there, that's what she'd say, "Let's have a little something," when my sister was tired of the magazines we read to her, or the chit-chat; when she'd yell at us to "Go away" because her headaches were constant, they had taken over her head, it was killing her when they took her off morphine. She swore and cursed at us, at the nurses, at the neurologist, especially at the orthopedic specialist, Mr. Jones. He got blasted every time. He told us it was the head injuries; it wasn't her.

But it definitely sounded like her.

I was so busy in Brighton, I had the hospital from nine a.m. until seven p.m., and even then she'd complain when I left that I was being selfish and didn't care. And then I tried to hold down a job because all the money I'd saved up to go around Europe was disappearing on scones, cups of tea, the twenty-seven pence bus fares. I got a job as Room Service waiter at the Grand Hotel, on night shift. I wore a suffocating penguin suit and worked from eleven p.m. till four a.m. I slept most of my shift. The few call-outs involved bottles of champagne to adulterous couples in sea-facing rooms who always tipped out of embarrassment. I held the heavy plastic trays in my slippery hands and exited the service elevator thinking, "Hit the ground running. Hit the ground running."

But here, in Rome, I am running underwater. I have no energy. I wake up and the only reason to get out of the single bed is the thought of *biscotti* for breakfast, dunked in sweet, milky cappuccino. I chat to Maria-Sylvania, the Portuguese housekeeper, but she just smiles and nods. She has lunch to make. And she misses her boy who lives with her mother near

Porto and she only sees four weeks per year. She has her own troubles. I can't put what I want to say into words. The thing about my mind.

I go out and take the orange bus and never pay, just to see if I will be caught. Sometimes I don't pay for all my Baci; I pay for some and pocket a few, to see if it will go noticed. I phone my sister, and she complains that I left her, left her to it with her legs still in their casts. Her legs have shrunk, she tells me when she gets the casts off; they have shriveled to sticks. I tell her I'll come see her for Christmas.

I go sit on the steps at Piazza di Spagna and stare into thin air.

At night, I hear noise from the wine bars in the street below and I want to climb out the window and down the drainpipe. I have no house keys and am too nervous to ask the Albaneses for them. I don't think the Albaneses want me to have house keys. Or go out. I roll over and go to sleep, I know I won't climb down.

In Brighton, at night I watched TV and ate a piece of toast for dinner and said hello to Cornelius, my sister's Dutch roommate who must've felt bad for her being run over and almost dying, but was probably sick of the relatives camping out in her room for months. He always asked, "How's she?" and I would report the medical facts. The skin grafts, the bone grafts, the healing this, and the knitting that. He nodded with optimism at all times. She didn't die. She came out of the coma kicking. "She's a tough one," Cornelius would say and head down to the pub.

I am letting down Rome. If my sister were here instead of

me she'd be doing it better. Even in leg casts, she'd curse at the jerks on the orange bus, flirt with the Baci vendors. She'd get house keys. She'd be down in that wine bar, meeting people, on crutches. She'd teach Signora Albanese a load of swear words in English. She would go further than Piazza di Spagna, further than the Vatican.

Betty or Alabama

"GOODNIGHT, SWEETIE!"

Cyb's parting words hung in the air as she fixed herself just one vodka and orange. Just only one, she told herself. Just for the Vitamin C. She felt that it was neither a good night nor that she was sweet. She felt hollow. Needing topping up. Ever so thirsty.

She looked at her coat, lying on the couch. She drifted into her bedroom. There was something hollow about it, too. A tourist's pit stop. Pacing back and forth in the hall, she saw something shoved under the front door. Funny. A piece of paper. She picked it up. The villa was freezing at this hour. She flicked on the bar heater and pulled Cyb's couch blanket over her. It was a note from Truman.

Darling Betty—I should call but I hate your roommate hearing any message. I was an idiot. I left my best brushes in your room and I really need them now. Can you drop them round sometime? I'm yours eternally if you could. Be a dear heart and do it before Friday, I have to finish a painting. Truman

She stared at her watch, ten to midnight. She drained the Screwdriver's dregs. Truman's paint brushes sat in the hall abandoned in rage as a symbol of Truman's disregard. She slipped into a coat, grabbed her bag, took the brushes and walked out, careful not to slam the door and wake Cyb. It was an open invitation, in her books, for anyone to pop round and see him. He wanted the brushes, didn't he?

All was dead still on Vermont Street, the moon cast pools of shadow, contorting tree branches into twisted people. She sped walked with her house keys threaded through her fingers in case someone jumped out from the bushes of fragrant Queen of the Night to attack. She learned self-defense at school—you punched into the face, aiming for the eyes, with the keys sprouting out like metal mini-javelins, then you kneed them in the groin and if they were still standing you grab their ears and violently head-butted and if you did that part right (smashing the front of your skull into nose bones) then you might even drive the bones upwards into his brain cavity and kill Bad Man instantly.

She hummed the procedure to herself as she zigzagged the street. She figured it was safer in the middle of the road. Lampposts only shed white light on about a quarter of the footpath. She had to go to the bottom of Vermont, along John Street bordering on the pitch black reserve that was plenty big enough to accommodate molesters, druggies, kids into petty theft and lecherous old assholes. To reach Truman's you went all along John up to Pompellier, then did a quick dog-leg into Clarence. His was number thirty-four. A two-bedroom bungalow where he lived alone. It was a seven house, in numerology, a fact that Truman used as an argument to never move in with any girlfriend—a seven was all about spirituality, a haven, an 'artistic' recluse. Cyb had waxed lyrical about house numerology from her book on palmistry, numerology, and other bullshit: the 'artistic' had to be in quotes because it was never included in the descriptions of house numerology. But Truman was adamant, if he lived in a seven house he lived there alone so he could create. Argument ensued, *What about you move then? A three house could be good, or what about a five?* Fruitless questions. He never even bothered giving a fruitless answer.

She turned right onto John Street.

There was a pink roofed house along here somewhere that she had always wanted to live in. She couldn't see it tonight. There were even fewer lampposts on John. An incline obscured what lay over the next rise. The dips in the street were deep and eerie. The footpaths were too skinny and cars choked the narrow road, some were alarmed, some were broken down shoddy things, one was lit up with people inside, smoking something. There was a party on somewhere near.

Over the rise, she heard the baseline of Dave Dobbyn at twenty paces. She never broke into tears at the sound of "Loyal."

She passed number sixty-nine, rundown with broken porch railings, patchwork lawn, and crumbling concrete fence. The front door was open and Dave was up full bore. People moved about inside, down the hall, across the hall, some stumbling, others holding cigarettes and drinks. Raucous laughter and insane cackling floated outside. It looked like a cross-section, from the bodies littering the front porch, of late teens to early forties. All white and pickled. No bros out here. The neighbors would try to shut them down in precisely forty minutes when noise control could act. One o'clock was the time when the noise police were authorized to drive round, knock politely on the door and ask that the volume on the stereo be "reduced dramatically." By then the guys on the broken sofas and three legged chairs outside would be clinging to each other singing the theme to *Footrot Flats*.

"Hey, honey, come in for a brew?" one lad called.

"Where you going? To paint a house?" another giggled. He'd spotted the paint brushes in her hand, being the witty observant type that he was. She waved in a blur, with her middle finger more prominent, a cheery way to say 'Up yours.' But so fast they wouldn't see it. Not with the amount of Steinlager in them.

"Not if you paid me," she said, but not low enough.

"What, you take money? Come on in!"

That wasn't a bright thing to say. She continued, shaking her head, eyes forward. No encouragement. She hoped they were just being drunk harmless mulled sheep. She had her mission. She held the paint brushes in her hand. Leave me alone, she radiated.

They didn't move off their decrepit furniture. She walked even faster. She was probably in the fat-burning zone by now. She was almost at the end of John, ready for the dog-leg. She took the corner, eyes scanning up and down for dangers. A car burned down Pompellier going too fast, it swerved around the traffic island. A Triumph 2500. Chocolate brown. Wide nose, low to the ground, a grunty car. The approaching cars headlights blinded her for a moment and the dark figure of a girl on the path must have spooked the driver—he over corrected coming out of the traffic island's narrow trajectory, his front right tire hooked up over the curb and shunted the car sideways, terribly close, causing a leap back against a hedge. He over corrected again and the back ass of the car swung out over to the other side of Pompellier and when he tried to get control back, he must have pumped the gas instead of brakes, a stupid reflex action, but one that caused the whole brown beast to spin 180, just miss a plane tree and run itself aground on the bonnet of a parked Japanese import about ten meters down the road. The buckled Triumph hissed, a huge sigh of disappointment in its driver, and shut down. Oil fanned out like life blood into the street. The crash hadn't made much noise. She dashed over to the car and reached for the driver's door.

It wasn't a guy, it was a woman driving. "How terrible to be a stereotype," she thought. Every male in New Zealand already had a thing against women drivers and here was another one to validate their lousy theory. She was almost angry at the woman, who turned the ignition key off with long red fingernails, and slowly reached for her seat belt. Her head was bleeding and her chin and forehead were cut from the shattered windscreen. She was a skinny brunette in her thirties, with dark hair all pulled up in a messy chignon, wearing too much Elizabeth Arden Red Door perfume and a loud charm bracelet clattering away on her cut wrist. Everywhere seemed a bit cut, blood seeped from different parts. It surprised her that the blood didn't make her feel anything. (Not like that time Cyb beat a mouse to death and she screamed in repulsion and terror.) She felt only this sense of being the strong one on this dark empty street.

"Let me help. Are you alright?"

She reached to help with the buckle. It was a dumb question, a dumb introduction to this woman, who clearly wasn't alright. Suddenly she thought about whiplash and broken spinal cords and paralysis and a big thought came to her: This Woman Cannot Be Moved.

A light went on in a nearby house. Then it flicked off. She looked around. For fuck's sake. This was surely why she should invest in a mobile phone. Now she'd have to go knocking on doors to call an ambulance. This woman would be paralyzed from the neck down if she was touched in any way, shape or form.

"I'm okay. I'm okay." The woman took her handbag from beside her and fumbled inside it. A lipstick was unearthed. Revlon ColorStay. The woman twisted the rear-view mirror towards her and held the lipstick up.

She gasped at her reflection. "Oh. No. Look. At. Me."

"Listen. Don't move. Just stay there. I'll go get someone to call an ambulance. Okay? Don't move."

The woman turned her head and finally acknowledged another human was there. "What? Oh. Okay."

She took off up the path of the nearest house that had cruelly turned its light on then off. She thought about maybe going back up John to that party to use their phone. But that would probably involve having a beer with them first to explain the 'Sit-chu-A-shon.' No time.

She knocked on the door. She looked down at the car with steam hissing. She knocked again. She still held the paint brushes in her hand. She looked down. The woman's blood was smeared down one arm of her denim jacket, where she'd reached in to undo the seat belt. Yuck. And where was the passing traffic? No cars out tonight? Not *one* car taking this shortcut through the back of Ponsonby on a Tuesday night after midnight? That figured. She knocked on the door harder. Finally, it opened.

An old geezer stood in his mental-ward-blue pajamas and paisley bathrobe, tied tight. He kept the door's safety chain on, a flimsy, piece of gold chain like a necklace promising lifelong love. He squinted through the gap. "What do you want?"

"This woman's had an accident. See?" Because he really ought to have figured that out already, unless he was completely deaf, "Can you call an ambulance? Please?"

"What's the number?" he asked, gruff and short.

Bless him. A geriatric with attitude. It would've been quicker to saunter down to the losers on the front porch couch and smoke a big doobie and let the woman walk herself home.

"God, I don't know! I think it's... 911! No, it's not 911. It's..." She had no idea. She'd never had to call an ambulance. All those stupid American TV shows were to blame. They'd gone and gotten imbedded in her brain—the American number for ambulances was all she could think of. "Call 0. Call the operator on 0 and ask them."

The old man squinted at her, his forehead wrinkled up like a dachshund's skin, like his heckles rising at the full moon, recoiling from the fully blown signs of insanity he figured he was facing down on his doorstep.

"Are you drunk, miss?"

"What? No. Listen. Just call the operator. Dial O. Get an ambulance. This Woman Cannot Be Moved!"

Without another word, the old geezer shut the door. Moments later his light switched off.

She could hear the car hissing away behind her. It wasn't like she was hallucinating, or making this shit up, the car crash was right there in plain view. Bastard. Where was his *humanity*? She turned, jumped up with adrenaline, grabbed a handful of ragged gravel from the guy's path and lobed it at his bay window. Nothing broke. More's the pity. She returned to the woman, who had half of her handbag spilled into her lap and was ferreting through her things, trying to find key evidence to destroy before she was carted away by the authorities, perhaps. She saw a phone among the detritus.

"Hey, you've got a phone! Okay. *We're* gonna call the ambulance."

The woman's fingers curled around the phone. She started sobbing, "No. I don't want to make any calls."

"What? Please. Just pass me the phone. I'll take care of it."

The woman snatched it away, hiding it down by the handbrake. She'd actually pulled the handbrake. It was up as far as it could go. The automatic transmission was still in 'D,' though. The phone was far from reach, with the woman bent over to protect it. The bare side of her stomach protruded from between her top and black trousers. She started dialing with her red nails that weren't even chipped. The blood still trickled from her chin and forehead. She held the phone up to her ear. To the good side of her head. The other side still bled and her hair was matted into another wound on the back of her head.

"Baby? Baby, it's me." The woman sobbed in an uncontrollable wail, like a five-year-old. "I've had an accident!"

She tried to reach for the phone, but the woman jerked away like the touch was sulfuric acid. This was so stupid.

The woman went on like a convulsed child, "Can you come get me? I don't know where I am…" More tears. Blood mixing with saline, her top turning pink.

She really wanted a double vodka now. She'd tried to help and look at this dumb cow. What a performance. "I'm in Ponsonby," the woman bawled, like Ponsonby was the other side of the universe, "I'm on…" The woman paused, eyes glazed and searching for a street name. "I'm on…" There was no sign.

She hollered, so the idiot on the other end might hear that a perfectly sane bystander was ready to communicate: "POMPELLIER TERRACE."

The woman shut her eyes, took another ragged breath, continued as if she'd had divine inspiration suddenly from above. "I'm on Pompellier Terrace." She added some extra awful whimpers and hung up.

Praise the Lord, help was on the way. Halle-fuckin'-luiah. She now saw a packet of cigarettes on the woman's lap, disgorged from her expensive-looking handbag. She asked, "Can I have a cigarette?"

The woman ignored her. She leaned down and grabbed the packet. All she wanted was one cigarette. She deserved it. She should've gone back up to that party on John Street and invited the boys to rip off this dumb woman's fancy car stereo, her wallet, and then steal her phone. She'd tried to help this woman, who now fumbled with the seat belt buckle again, attempting to go for a walk, and look at the ingratitude flung in her face.

"You think you can walk, then?" She took out one solitary cigarette and the lighter stuffed into the packet and stepped away from the car in case gas fumes combusted them both. She lit the Dunhill Blue, and inhaled deeply before tossing the packet back onto the woman's lap.

"I think it would be better if you just wait in the car for your 'baby' to come collect you. Since you declined an ambulance. You might have broken legs or damage to your spinal column. You might have *whiplash*, lady."

Sure, she sounded petulant by this stage—she didn't exactly mean to come across all sarcastic. She wondered what was the story with this woman. Why she refused an ambulance? It was as if she'd stolen the car. And who was 'Baby'? Odd. All of it. And as for the golden oldie... She cast her eye at his letterbox: number 43. Another seven house. A haven. Don't go knocking on the door. No visitors admitted. She held the paint brushes between her ribs and her arm while she smoked the cigarette. It was so cold. She checked her watch. Five to one. How did it get so late? Finally, a sign of life: a man called out, racing toward the car, a tall figure wrapped up in a gigantic marl gray duffel coat. Even with black wool pulled over his forehead she knew him: Truman.

"Baby? Baby! Are you alright?" He reached the car and pulled the woman into his arms. Practically yanked her out the car like he was the Jaws of Life.

She hid now, frozen, hidden under the twisted-people shadows of the plane trees. The paint brushes slid down the crack between her arm and her body. She heard them rattle to the ground. Truman?

"Oh, Baby." And suddenly the sobbing, crazy bitch came to life and went on and on about how nobody came to help her and she had had to call him to come himself and she couldn't believe nobody even called an ambulance. She stepped forward. Truman supported the woman so she could walk. The woman's arms flopped about—pure melodrama—her arms weren't broken, nothing of the sort. Truman soothed her, saying he'd called a tow-truck and the car could be fixed—and that it would be okay now, now that he was there. Cooing like a stupid pigeon that everything would be fine.

She opened her mouth, "Hey!"

He swiveled. The woman hung off his arm like a shopping bag.

"Hey, what are you doing here?" He didn't even sound grateful. He sounded annoyed.

"What am I doing? What are *you* doing? Are you seeing that bitch? Tell me you're not."

Truman stared—up and down—eyes confused. "Were you in the car?"

"Of course not. I was walking over to return your brushes. She practically ran me over having her stupid accident! She's a terrible driver."

The woman said, "I need to lie down, Baby!"

He gripped around her waist tighter and turned away, "I'm going to take care of you. Don't you worry." He led her around the corner but their voices carried in the cold, still night. The woman started up with, "Who was that?" and Truman replied, "Nobody—forget about it." "What was she doing out here at this time of night? Is she crazy?" and Truman said nothing.

She picked up the paint brushes and felt the smooth blonde wood between her fingers, noting they had authentic and dangerous-looking smears of blood on them now. She walked up to the old man's letterbox: number 43 and shoved the brushes through the slit. A present for a kindly old man. Now she was happy that the old codger hadn't helped that woman. The music from the party could be heard: "Loyal." It inexplicably *did* make her tear up. A tow truck appeared in the street like an avenging *deus ex machina*.

"Someone called for a tow?"

"Yes. Take it to the wreckers," her voice sounded miles away to her ears. Like she was speaking from another country.

"Doesn't look totaled to me."

"It's a bad luck car now. Better to destroy it completely."

The man started scribbling in the forms. "And who do I send the bill to?"

She recited Truman's name and address. Scrawled her signature to authorize the wreckers to crush the Triumph into a metal box. Right on time, the noise police swung around the corner—the same corner that the women failed to negotiate—on their way to turn down the party. She trailed after the police car back the way she'd come, at a zombie's pace. She threaded her house keys through her fingers again to ward off attack from a Bad Man.

Betty

"LATE ON THE RENT again. Plus this."

If she didn't move this might only be a nightmare. Shadowy figures stood over her bed. Paper rustled. Betty remained fetal, cheek to pillow, eyes stapled shut.

"She was supposed to go pay the electricity yesterday. I just rang. She didn't." Cybelline foghorned.

"For sure she'll pay the late payment fee." Alabama's voice had the singsong cadence of someone still affected by the night before.

Cyb sat on the end of the bed. "It's more than always being late with the rent. Look at the state of her. What time did you girls get home last night?"

"It wasn't so late," Alabama drawled.

Betty opened her eyes a crack, taking in her red Mickey Mouse alarm clock. His gloved hands pantomimed: 10:08 A.M. She had work at eleven. She rolled onto her back and looked at her two roommates.

"What is this? Barging into my room when I'm asleep?"

Cyb bounced deliberately on the bed. She had a face like a Modigliani and a body like Barbie. The incongruities of Cybelline Harper didn't stop there. She was fickle, maternal, exacting and the oldest of the three roommates. Cyb was known for three things: being a devoted maître d', her party trick of getting her own nipple into her mouth, and the fact that she rarely wore underwear beneath her skin-tight dresses, even while serving food. But her name was on the lease.

"I'm calling a vote to kick you out of the house," Cyb's mocha eyes squinted.

Betty struggled into her red satin dressing gown plucked off the floor.

"I'm voting you go," Cyb continued. "And you, Alabama?"

Betty's blood thudded and her bedroom spun in a kaleidoscope of shame. Chicken-coop wardrobe, bookshelves stuffed with university tomes, small fake-zebra couch suffocated by dirty laundry, clean and unclean garments dumped on the unpainted floorboards, thin curtains perpetually half-mast, and a wooden desk made from wine crates littered with dust-bunnied paper.

"Well, I vote I stay," Betty said. "In my defense, I got caught up and forgot about the electricity bill. But I'll pay everything today."

Betty remembered telling Alabama last night that she had precisely $40 left in her account until they got paid next Tuesday. That was when Ruben started buying them rounds of those nasty shots.... what were they called again? Quick Oblivion? She shuddered.

"You owe $290, sweetie. The late rent, your share of the electricity, plus the late payment fee," Alabama said softly.

Betty swallowed hard. Alabama was a girl who paid everything a day in advance.

Cyb boomed, "Your vote, Alabama?"

Alabama's velvety eyes flickered in hesitation. She swayed a little, her platinum blonde pageboy all-askew and her white terrycloth bathrobe mussy. Definitely looking still drunk, to Betty's trained eye. "I'm sure Betty'll pay it all."

"Matthew will go spare if we're late again." Cyb said. "I can stall a day, or two, but…"

"By Saturday I'll definitely have it all. No problem," Betty grabbed for the extra time.

"We reassess Saturday then," Cyb nodded, satisfied that her message had impregnated Betty's addled brain. Alabama wandered out (probably to throw up, very quietly).

Their 'fourth roommate' by default, Laverne, snuck in, squatted over the remains of Betty's black clothes—her black mini that might have stood up to one more day's wear—pissing her fat, calico heart out.

Betty grabbed Laverne to stop her in mid-stream of conscious piss. But the skirt was already soaked.

Laverne was in the tenancy agreement: "One Laverne, to be cared for in exchange for cheap rent" stipulated by Matthew Mayer, owner of the villa they rented on Vermont Street, Ponsonby, Auckland, before he emigrated to the south of France. Matthew was disturbingly firm on the Laverne Clause and regularly requested photos of her sitting on *The New Zealand Herald* with the date showing, to prove the cat was still alive.

"I swear I'm going to machete that sack of mange," Betty said as Laverne scrambled to Cyb, blunt claws splintering.

Cyb snorted, "As if. Remember the mouse? You two screamed your heads off while I bashed it with that broom."

"Yeah, while this fleabag did nothing instead of catching the mouse in the first place."

"She only pees in your room. Maybe she wants you gone."

"You don't really want me gone. You'd miss me. Friends don't do that."

"Friends also don't piss all over their responsibilities," Cyb lifted the wet skirt with her pinkie. "Let me put this through a wash for you. Got anything else to go in?"

"Everything," Betty gathered up two armfuls of black clothes and trudged down the hall. She was due at work in thirty minutes. "God... I'm on a double today and I was going to wear that skirt... and I've got no black tops left, could I maybe borrow your long Glory dress or your Marilyn Sainty shirt dress?"

Cyb shoved the dirty washing in the machine, sprinkled Persil and yanked the knob out to start the cycle with an ear-splitting Pop! "Come into my room."

Betty leaned against the doorframe as Cyb contemplated outfits in her immaculate dressing room of her lace-trimmed, antique-decorated, four-poster lair. Cyb had been in a foul mood (complete with the boring, sermon-ridden streak) ever since she and her ex-boyfriend Vince (head chef down at Hasta Manana Baby) spontaneously combusted. Vince taking out a restraining order to protect himself from Cyb's Let's-Be-Friends antics hadn't exactly helped.

"If you had decent tits you could wear this," Cyb held up a plunging V-neck vintage number.

"I'm on a double," Betty countered. "Nobody wants a plunging neckline at lunch."

"They do at my place of work," Cyb mused, holding up other options to Betty's neck.

"You'd never kick me out, you love dressing me too much," Betty joked, weak-kneed. Did something happen to her knees last night? She peeked under the dressing gown—yep, black and blue with bits of gravel still embedded.

"Holy hell, what did you do to yourself?"

"The driveway," Betty confessed.

Cyb busied about with tweezers, cotton wool, and Dettol.

"See, you wouldn't kick me out, you'd have nobody to mother," Betty tried to joke while gripping the doorframe to stay vertical. She knew if she sat—or worse, lay down—at this stage she'd never get up.

Cyb refused to look at her. "There was another rape, you know—on Islington Street. Night before last. Jeez, Betty, you and Alabama get home at God-knows-what time most nights—certainly after two a.m. when I get home from work, leaving me alone here night after night. *I could be next.* If you're not at home by 1.55 from now on then I'll get a man to move in who will be."

"You're not going to be raped, Cyb. You're a black belt in karate."

"He uses a knife. He breaks bones. This is his tenth attack. They're calling him 'The Psychic' because he seems to know when women are alone at home. We can't get a dog with the Laverne Clause. Fuck it, Betty, the only reason I've been keeping you in the house is out of loyalty to our friendship. Do you get it now?"

"Okay, okay."

Cyb pushed her black Glory dress and a pair of tights into Betty's hands.

"Borrow these for today," she herded Betty towards the shower. "And come straight home after work."

"I will."

"And you need that $290."

"I'm sorry, Cyb. I'm going to do better."

"If you're quick I can give you a lift on my way to work."

"Two secs."

But in the shower, a rush of red vertigo engulfed her and she threw up bile that sluiced down the plughole along with the stale sweat, make-up, and cigarette smoke. Lithgow talked about the serial rapist earlier this week. He knew one of the victims; she lived alone in Grey Lynn. She'd been tied up at knifepoint, raped, then made to drive up deserted John Street to the cash machine near Williamson to take out all the cash she possibly could to give him, then made to drive back to her flat where she was raped again. She had a broken arm, collapsed lung, and not even a description as he'd worn a balaclava and gloves and kept the room pitch black. Nobody saw them. She'd wanted to crash the car to get away from him, but was too scared she'd do it wrong and break her own neck, as he wore a seat belt but she wasn't allowed to wear hers and her crappy Ford Escort had no airbag.

Despite the glitch of a head that felt like it had been slammed in a refrigerator, Betty weaved between packed tables with trays and plates seemingly glued to her forearms. Being an extraordinary waitperson.

She addressed Table five: eight thirty-somethings on a

friends' night out.

"Are you ready to order?"

"What were those specials again?" asked Alpha Male.

La Bohème's "Mi chiamano Mimì" climbed in volume around them. Betty twisted her knife around the neck of a 1994 Santa Margherita Pinot Grigio.

"Tonight our pasta is giant squid linguini with poached lime infusion; our fish is Blind Bay cray grilled with pimento parmesan served on a mattress of artichoke and tamarillo; and as a main we have braised lamb shanks propped by a medley of roasted radicchio, parsnip, and celeriac with a prune infusion and swimming in a Valpolicella glaze. Would you like to taste the Pinot Grigio, sir?"

Betty dispensed the usual teaser, which the man sniffed at, chewed over, and grimaced. She doubted he would even be able to tell if the wine was corked. Italian whites tasted weird anyway to Kiwi palates.

"Not bad. I think we're ready."

A system operates in any well-reviewed restaurant that reduces every patron to a number so other members of staff can deliver food and drinks without having to ask *who had what*. To ask *who had what* was a cardinal sin for hospos: workers in the restaurant/café/bar industry who took quality of service deadly seriously. Betty would rather gnaw her left arm off than have to ask *who had what*. Table five commenced calling out their orders indiscriminately, but to Betty they each turned into a number and two or three keywords. Nothing would be written down until she reached the bar and wrote out the order in triplicate.

"I'll have the oysters, then the duck, but can I have it with no sauce?"

"Same, but with the sauce, and no entrée."

"Or do you want to share the tempura with me?"

"Sure, okay."

"And I'll have the guinea fowl for my main, thank you."

"Uh, I'd like the antipasta followed by an entrée-sized special linguini..."

"Are you sure you can eat giant squid when you're pregnant?"

"Good point, I probably shouldn't... uh... come back to me."

"And another bottle of this stuff, it's not too shabby."

"Uh, and another apple juice, no ice, please."

"I just want an Antipasto with no olives as my main, hon."

"I'll have the scallops, then that crayfish you mentioned. Unless you guys are keen on a red later?"

"I'm definitely up for red."

"Then I'll have a steak instead of the cray."

"How would you like that cooked?" Betty asked.

"Overeasy, ha! No, medium rare. Aren't you writing this down?"

Everyone stopped and realized that Betty was flying solo. Not scribbling down a single letter of their order. She was also pouring wine and water alternately with her left and right arms. She was a waitress savant and ambidextrous. Some panicked. One frowned.

Betty smiled, "It's fine, and what would you like, sir?"

"The tureen then the lamb shanks, please."

"Same."

"Uh, I'll have the veal as my main, entrée-sized, if possible."

"Oh, can I change? I'll have the veal, too, normal-size."

And then one of the sunbed-orange wives tried to make it easy: "And a couple of green salads for the table?"

Betty smiled and harvested the menus. She wrote up their order perfectly on triple-copy paper dockets that she dispensed to bar and kitchen. There had been talk of getting that new-fangled computer system to put the orders through, but Dean Staples, the owner of Marble, was strictly old-school. And a miser. So, everything went through a waitress's head and then onto paper.

The head chef, Gabriel Cumming, glanced at the docket, snarling, "Come back for 14's mains."

Gabriel had a body as tight as Michelangelo's *David* (but hopefully with a penis in proportion), perpetual stubble, and dangerous eyebrows. His twenty-six years was a perfect counterpart to her twenty-two. Betty paused and ventured a smile. She had a crotch-burning crush on him.

"What part of 'Come back' don't you understand?" He turned to flame a skillet of ribs.

But she held few illusions of them becoming a couple; his anger intrigued her.

Betty collected drinks from Tom, who was away with the fairies tonight. He'd put ice in the pregnant woman's apple juice. Now, Tom was real eye-candy behind the bar, but his occasional slip-ups meant he was still a debutant hospo and *that* wasn't sexy. He was a surfer at core, with sunfried hair and the intriguing scent combo of Old Spice, vegetarian sweat, and marijuana. He made appropriate small talk with regulars, crushed ice by hand for his cocktails, and filled out orders with admirable determination, but the joint he smoked nightly meant he sometimes forgot the basics. A true hospo wouldn't.

"Uh, Tom? It's written 'No ice' buddy..."

She waited while he fished out the offending cubes and topped up, slurping her flat soda water and cracking her neck from side to side. A body memory of knocking back shots of, what was it?—Jägermeister?—left her awash with queasiness. Tom replaced the apple juice on her tray.

"Cheers, my dear."

She deposited drinks to table five who now stared at her like she was the goddess of service. Nobody noticed her hands tremble as she opened their second white.

La Bohème kicked up to Mimì and Rodolfo's getting-it-on music. Betty hummed out back to load up table 14's mains.

"Compliments from six on the shanks," she told Gabriel. "The woman said she died and went to heaven on your glaze."

"Tell her I've got another glaze back here she can have. The one in my cock. That. She. Can. Suck."

He gave her a truly demented grin. Inwardly, she swooned but her unimpressed eyebrow raise didn't drop.

"Take this," hissed Petal, the larder chef, shoving 14's side orders at her. He then grabbed the salad back to tweak the top leaves of rocket as if they were nipples to be clamped. Petal was a perfectionist who moved fast and furiously over his small bowls. He got more height on his tempura vegetable entrées than any other larder chef in Marble's history of service. Six inches, easy.

"I'm going on three's mains then five's entrées," Gabriel yelled.

Betty spun, "You mean me?"

Petal spat in fury, "No, me!"

"Out!!!! You're fucking my flow!" Gabriel hollered.

By half past midnight, the restaurant had thinned to one last table of stubborn diehards clinging to their ports in the opera storm. Table five had left at eleven-thirty—loud, rowdy and full (apart from the pregnant one who complained of heartburn). Despite the faultless service, they'd tipped a measly $20 on a bill of $460. Friends on a couples' night out were never good tippers. Business people and Americans were the good tippers. Table five thanked Betty prosaically, but their tab wasn't on an expense account and wives get shitty if hubbies tip a lot unless one of the wives was a former hospo and understood how hard Betty worked.

The two businessmen left on table eight glanced up. Betty scurried over. Florence Nightingale in an apron.

"Two espressos. And the bill, thanks."

"And a couple of taxis."

"And, hell, why not one last port for the road, eh?"

"Certainly, sirs," Betty smiled.

The trick with businessmen was to make it look like you never wanted them to leave—ever. That you'd happily make up a bed for them by the log fire and read them a bedtime story, if asked. At Marble, half the regulars were there on business. They strode into the great green room with a glow of anticipation of getting tanked on the vast selection of New

Zealand and imported wines; of savoring the Italian fusion; of witty chitchat and spot-on wine matches with Nikki and her troupe. They were never disappointed.

Table eight finally rose to leave after their taxis had waited outside for fifteen dollars' worth, weaving a little, calling to Betty their affected farewells. She helped them into their coats and the taller man pressed a fifty into her palm.

"Top meal, Betty, cheers," the shorter one said.

"Glad you had a good night, gentlemen."

As soon as they were gone, Betty changed the music from Verdi to Garbage. She wiped down the vacant marble tables, scratching melted candle wax off with her blunt nails as she soaped down. Her reflection shimmered in the gilt-edged mirror over the fireplace: pale, bloodshot blue eyes and black ringlets. By Sunday she would very likely be kicked out of her home of the last three years, as the likelihood of making $290 in tips in the next 48 hours was awfully slim. That fact hurt. Nikki, the restaurant manager, sat at the bar hunched over a glass of Pinot Noir, tallying tips. Betty slapped the fifty on the pile.

"They practically proposed marriage."

"Good girl."

"I'm done," Betty gutted her white apron of her trusty wine knife and dozens of wine bottle foils and threw it expertly into the laundry bag of stinking kitchen cloths.

Nikki was a workhorse of thoroughbred pedigree. She partnered with Dean Staples (the most ill-tempered owner/ chef imaginable) to create Marble from a former meat storage depot near Auckland downtown harbor—turning a sheep morgue into an emerald arena of opulence. It was her lifeblood and Nikki spent ninety hours a week on this floor. Guesses on her age ranged from thirty to fifty; she was without a line, tall and sinewy, a one-time model turned hospitality diva, oozing glamour even as she charged across the floor to deliver drinks. Tough as over-chewed Nicorette, Nikki was Betty's touchstone to reality and a martyr to boot. She poured Betty's one free after-service glass of wine, pausing, as if scenting the air for vodka departing pores via osmosis. With one mouthful, Betty felt human again with the thick, liver-corroding red running through her veins. Nikki eyed her.

"Pull up a pew, hon." Subtext: *Drop and give me 20.*

"I'm beat. Looking forward to blobbing in front of the telly." Subtext: *I may have to go out and get blotto.*

"You're amazing, hon, you came in today looking like you'd been scraped out of bed, but you still make great tips." That was literal.

"They were lovely customers today," Betty stalled. Golden rule: never admit you were out all night, even when your double shift was over. Nikki could tell Betty had walked in that day with an excruciating hangover; she just played dumb to it because Nikki never mollycoddled.

"I need you to up your shifts."

"I'm already on eight." Betty never liked the Nikki Guilt Trip. That's how she'd gone from five shifts per week during university to becoming a fulltime waitperson with apparently no other prospects.

"Ten. I need you on permanent doubles Thursdays and Fridays. Elodie's done her back in."

"Bloody Elodie. She's useless. From when?"

"Tomorrow."

"Okay, okay."

"I'm loving your sense of team spirit here."

"It's fine, I was going to ask for an extra shift tomorrow. I'm behind on some housekeeping pin money."

"How behind?"

"I need $290," Betty gnawed her thumbnail. Would Nikki loan it to her?

"Hhmm," Nikki said coolly. "Make sure you don't spend your tips on black Sambucas, then, hon."

"Okay, okay."

Betty pocketed her tip money: $112,50. Tips were shared equally between waitresses, with 25 percent going to the bar and kitchen. Betty knew that she personally had pulled in $240, which meant Elodie, the other waitress on today, had sucked. On a good double she could make around $180. The $290 was still possible. Maybe.

The restaurant phone rang. One guess.

"Hey there," came the sultry tones.

"Alabama! What's up?"

"We are *so* making sure you get together that $290 for Cyb, right? But are you up for a quiet one at Eros?"

Betty hesitated. It was half past midnight and Cyb wanted her and Alabama home before two a.m. That gave them plenty of time for one drink. "Sure. But just one," she breathed into the phone.

"I'll swing by in two ticks."

Nikki's X-ray vision burned holes in the back of her head.

"Alabama's on her way home so she's giving me a lift," Betty explained.

"Be in at eleven. We're already fully booked for lunch and dinner," Nikki said. "No antics, you got it? Especially if you're in trouble with rent, hon."

"Of course. It's not rent... it's mainly electricity."

"It's still trouble. Don't blow it."

Now Lithgow takes a Polaroid from his duffel bag, taking snapshots of you resting your fringe on the bar. Lithgow's your best male buddy, purely platonic, always ready with a quip, never judging, happy-go-lucky, fellow struggler to pay rent, fellow not-eating-right, and binge drinker. With Lithgow you've discussed openly how much you drink and he drinks and you tell each other it's best to live in the present and forget the past, forget the future.

Click, whirr.

You're in Eros with Lithgow. Alabama's one barstool away. The big ol' clock behind the bar says last round—ten to two. You calculate that's still enough time to get home and appease Cyb. Keep her safe from all those rapist nasties out there

Click, whirr.

"How are you, really, pet?"

"I've been holier. Going through a phase, I think."

Click, whirr.

"What sort of phase?"

"Sort of a get-bad, get-deliberately-worse sort of phase."

"But you're creating art. These are beautiful, pet. Look."

You put the three pretty Polaroids in a side pocket of the leather mini backpack that you got on sale in High Street. You've spent $0 of that $112,50—those efforts of your smile—because everyone's buying Betty a drink tonight in solidity (solidarity?). You are a charity case with your quest for two-nine-zero. You are a Telethon. Three vodka tonics, four Tequila Mocking Babe shots, a half-bottle of champagne (gift from Johnny Tender, owner of Eros) a Strawberry Daiquiri gifted by some random guy with diabolical hair. But no inebriation, dear soul, only pleasant haziness. You dive into your next vodka tonic with gusto as Johnny Tender places a free shot of Baileys and vodka beside your glass.

"Well, well, well: Miss Betty Asphalt."

Betty knew the voice before she even spun on her fake tiger-fur barstool. Truman. She instinctively straightened Cyb's black Glory dress, pulling it down over her opaque-stockinged legs. Truman was back. Truman was back and hadn't called. Her heart hurt like it was being squeezed in a Chinese burn and she could no longer breathe. Truman was back and hadn't called... so all that talk of them breaking up because he was going overseas and 'couldn't commit to a long-distance relationship even though he loved her more than life itself' was... bullshit. Truman was back and *didn't love her* and that tiny pilot light that flamed inside her was snuffed out. He turned, registered her presence, raised his glass in cheers, and turned away.

Truman was back and not even apologizing. Alabama was already on her feet dragging Betty away.

Outside in Vulcan Lane, they hopped and bobbed,

insufficiently dressed. Stamping their feet. It was June. Six degrees Celsius. Alabama checked her watch.

"We need to call it a night."

Betty nodded, her teeth chattering. Her cheeks were streaked red, her black ringlets limp and sodden as lamb's dags, and she kept looking over her shoulder. Alabama's starlet blonde, chin-length bob led the way like the tip of a fairy's wand, illuminating their path up Queen Street past drunken idiots and the occasional girl clinging to some animal she thought she was in love with. A light drizzle iced them. They headed for the taxi stand on the corner of Victoria Street because Alabama had a strict no-driving-drunk policy and always left her trusty Lada in the Shortland Street parking lot to collect the following morning.

Boy racers hooned up and down in their souped-up Cortinas with dirty rap blasting from stereos perhaps stolen. Asian kids got beat up round here. Pimps sold girls a few streets down on Fort Street. Usually they had a burly male to escort them from bar to bar or taxi at two in the morning. They didn't usually walk around by themselves. They had their buddies: Lithgow, Rick-o-Rick, Big Ruben and his troupe, Glenno, or Crazy Angus. Sweet guys who could be counted on to get you from A to B unmolested. The trouble was: there was no such thing as an available taxi on a Thursday at five minutes to two a.m. on the corner of Victoria and Queen in 1996.

They stood under a halogen nimbus at the void taxi stand. Extremity-chilling drizzle numbed their brains. Betty's ringlets went all flaccid on themselves. They stomped their boots some more.

"You okay?"

Betty shook her head, eyes leaking now. "Fucking Truman. I need a drink."

And Dragon Bar would welcome them with open arms.

Alabama has been temporarily misplaced. But it's not over.

"How about a Slippery Nipple?" Big Ruben says.

Like it's no big deal. Of course, it always is with Ruben. Dolling out endless fifties to keep you. You'll go to the toilets, take one look, think: 'I Must Go Home Now.' But you'll get it together, make it back to the bar, and Ruben will be there, smiling, another shot already lined up.

You slur. "Now, Ruben, ruby ruby. I really must decline."

"Don't say such things. A cleansing shot. One for the road."

"Of what?"

"Oh, it's called a Blow Job."

"Alright, but a blowjob is hardly cleansing."

"Just swallow, Betty."

"Wassa time?"

"Okay, we're going to Nirvana, right? Are you with me?"

"Sure, but where's Alabama?"

"God knows."

"I really think."

"Okay, so we'll see you there, okay, Betty Babe? At Nirvana?"

"Sure, but where's Alabama?"

The big hand and the little hand are on top of each other around the number four and Alabama's still lost.

"Where'd she go?"

The male beside you contemplates, "Maybe over to Nirvana?"

That's right, there had been talk. The nasty grotto. Final usual destination.

Finding Alabama. Alabama's swilling away, happy as a clam. In her ocean. The floor tilts like a seabed. Switch to mineral water.

Cold air. Pre-dawn shades of blue and pink. A taxi drives towards you. Lit up! You and Alabama flag madly.

It pulls over.

You leap in and sink into the unforgiving cold leather...

"That you again, girlie?" a voice says.

It says Baza on his plastic identity card and you and Baza know each other as of last night with the tumbling-on-gravel incident because before the tumbling you had a delightful chat about what you both wanted to be when you grew up.

"What are yous doing out so late again? Bloody oath, what time do you call this to be going home?"

Alabama giggles, "What's with?"

"C'mon, Mista Baza... it's all my ex's fault, Truman, he's such a jerk, he deserves a bullet thru his smug mug—honest."

Baza shakes his head. "Isn't you cold in no coat, girlie?"

You left your coat somewhere? Funny, hadn't felt a thing.

"I just don't get why yous is out so late. Why don't yous go home at a decent hour?"

"Why's it to you?"

"Yous girls don't see the streets like I see them. It's not

safe. It's six o'clock in the frickin' morning."

"It is? Shit."

"Mister Baza, you're getting us home safe," Alabama yawns.

"Yeah, we're safe."

"How bloody old are yous? Nineteen?"

"I'm twenty-two," you say.

Alabama, being nineteen, stumm. Legal age to drink here is her next birthday.

"Yous is babies."

"How old are you, then, Mister Baza?" Alabama drawls.

"Thirty-two."

"I put you at 23-25 tops!" Alabama says. "You are *so* wearing that well."

You say nothing. Gone too far. A bit too gone. Images of Truman still spinning in your muddled, hurt mind. Cold panic about the $290 and the hour. Cyb will kill you. Nikki will crucify you. You need to be at work in just under five hours. Except, now you've gone quiet you have a horrible feeling that you want to vomit. Not good in a taxi. There is the $80 fine to consider and you don't want to get on the wrong side of this guy, what's his ID say again? Baza. Nope. Must maintain stomach contents. Only another three streets. You're at the top of Franklin now. Turning left. Okay. Not long. Just the awful traffic islands and speed humps, and... a surge of vomit erupts from deep and you clamp your hands over your mouth.

"You better not be sick back there," Baza's eyes are on red alert, "You little bitch!"

More traffic islands. Vomit thick in your mouth, puffing

out your cheeks that grow tight and sore with the pressure. You are that First Chinese Brother who swallowed the sea. Alabama is concerned to your left. "We'll walk from here!"

Baza swerves to the curb.

"Get out, you bitches."

You can no longer control the sea of vomit, your stomach heaves and Baileys-scented puke projectiles straight over the passenger seat headrest to splatter the windscreen, Baza's ID, and his rubber dash ornaments on springs. There's not a drop on you. Or Alabama. You can't even taste it in your mouth. But the rubber puppy, dolphin, and clown all *drip*. You crawl out the backdoor throwing $80 plus $10 for the fare on the seat. Oh Lord, now you have only $22.50 of the $290.

You hear only the squeal as he pulls away.

Alabama and you are running now, as fast as your zombie legs will take you, giggling, get the key in the bastard keyhole, turn, in!!!! Shut door, lock, lock, chain. You lurch to the toilet. Yesssssssssssssssssssssssss, relief. Cyb's closed the shower curtain for some silly reason. You have an urge to peek behind the trendy black plastic. But don't. Must—bed.

And there everything stops; your brain ticks off and there is a fetal amniotic peace.

Another entity slips into the room. A squat furry body huddles, letting bladder fly.

She awoke to Cybelline's heavy stomping from the kitchen down the hall past her bedroom. The wooden floorboards reverberated in Betty's head. But she wasn't technically hung over. It was the way Cyb walked that hurt. And the yelling that accompanied it. Shit, that meant an Inverse Hangover was coming. Where you wake up feeling sort of okay and feel progressively worse as the day goes on. Mickey Mouse's hands pantomime 10:02 a.m. Ex-cell-ent. Plenty of time to get to Marble for 11:00.

"Come on! I'm not even giving her until Saturday. She's out today."

Alabama's reply was too feeble to be heard. Betty rolled onto her back, testing out her limbs. Nope, not exactly hung over, just terribly parched. Maybe, still drunk? Or perhaps she was blessed—throwing up in Baza's taxi had cleared all alcohol from her system? Then her foot collided with a leg. She recoiled. Peeked under the duvet.

Truman lay dead beside her—his face a ghoulish grimace, drool dried and flecked red, his throat slit, congealed, dark red, sticky.

Betty leaped out of the bed with an endless shriek pulling the duvet with her, to reveal all of Truman's naked, pale-green inert death pose. Cybelline and Alabama catapulted into the room.

And that was the end of a lot of things.

Stephanie

I GO TO KAIKOURA because the whale watching was on our list of holiday "musts." The only thing I managed to book was a spot on the boat at 7.15 tomorrow morning. After that all mobile signal dried up coming over the Ranges.

Black, chilly rain drives down. This is the middle of summer for God's sake. No wonder I left this country. I pull up outside the first motel's office and dash inside.

The guy cracks his knuckles, "Did you book ahead?"

"No, we had no chance."

He bursts into high-pitched laughter, "You got that right, you've got no chance. This here's the busiest time of the year, right? Them whales is having a bloody field day off the coast. Everything's booked up solid-as."

"Where's our best bet to try?"

"Check out the motels along the main drag. Or try the pink place."

The pink place. I trawl the main street with its one Kentucky Fried Chicken (burnt out by arson—temporarily closed), one petrol station (also closed now it's after seven o'clock), one teashop still serving, and half a dozen motels all with a big neon "NO" illuminated before "VACANCIES." In the streets behind are bed & breakfasts with jaunty little "No" signs hung out before "Rooms." I don't see the pink place until the sixth drive-by, when a moving body catches my eye and I see a guy running around his front room with no curtains to give him any privacy. There's a small sign saying B&B and the house is hot pink, so I pull in.

The rain hoses down on me while the asshole takes his sweet time opening the sliding door. In nylon running shorts, jandals, and a red and black Swan-Dri, he continues eating his baked beans cold from the tin.

"Did you book ahead?"

I shake my head, water droplets fly.

"Petey, do we still have that room?" he hollers and a giant of a man comes through a fly curtain; he's also in running shorts and a Swan-Dri but with gumboots, and he looks me up and down and says, "Did you book ahead?"

"We had no signal all day on our mobile."

He snorts like that's a great joke and says, "We got a room."

I've already decided I'd rather curl up and asphyxiate in the boot of the rented Ford Mondeo than sleep under these guys' roof and risk getting murdered in my sleep. I think of Emmanuelle, who I dragged to this part of the world, assuring her of the South Island's beauty and the dolphins and whales, and how amazing New Zealand is compared to up-itself Paris with its pollution and people in your face all day. She agreed in the beginning of the trip, down in Queenstown, but by Fox Glacier she'd turned, saying it was all freaks here, "Why'd you ever leave this 'aven of peace, Stephanie? This paradise?" she said in her sarcastic tone that I hated so much, exhaling smoke even though I explained the no-smoking rule for the rental.

"How much?" I ask.

The littler one says, "One fifty, including breakky." He chomps another spoonful of beans and some tomato sauce drips onto his Swan-Dri. He scrapes the sauce off and licks the spoon.

"Well, a hundred and fifty's a bit steep for us. We'll keep looking. Cheers though." I run for the car, hitting central lock and turn the music up way loud. Fat Boy Slim calms me down and I think of big nights out in London with Emmanuelle over for the weekend, and how beautiful they are—that cusp around three a.m. when you're still out and everyone around you is sparkling and laughing and you're having the time of your life and you know you'll never go back, you'll never need to go back, where nothing sparkles and every thing's dull, gray, and small.

The rain is vertical sleet now. The wipers can't keep up. Defrost is struggling. I head up a hill, aimless. In the pitch black I search for one Godforsaken sticker from one Godforsaken association that regulates Bed & Breakfasts in this Godforsaken shitsville with their damn whales.

I'm about to give up and drive out of town, up the coast to Marlborough Sounds, to vineyards full of Sauvignon Blanc, drive all night in circles if I have to, when I see a small sign still out, jangling in the storm: "ROOMS TO LET."

A large woman opens the door, wearing a white plastic apron and circus-red lipstick. She looks like a school dental hygienist.

"Do you have a room?"

"You didn't book ahead, did you, dear?"

"No."

"Well, I *do* have a room. Come on in. This rain is fearsome. I'm Val."

Her doormat reads I LOVE NEW ZEALAND in red, white and blue. A powerful smell of baked bran muffins hits.

"Now," Val starts, all business, "the room's one hundred dollars, including breakfast, and evening snacks. Cash only, I'm afraid. I've been the victim of check fraud in the past. People aren't well in this world."

She shows me a room upstairs. It screams floral, two twin beds pushed together with a synthetic floral bedcover in blue and pink. Floral lampshades, floral wallpaper, thick green carpet with round floral rug. I press the bed; it jiggles.

"The little boys 'n' girls' room is next door. The amenities are shared, I'm afraid. Downstairs I've installed a water dispenser—come down any time of the night for water. You won't disturb me, no fear, I sleep in the back room with my cats."

"I'll take it."

Val stops, studying me.

"Where are you from, my dear?"

"London, but I live in France now. In Paris."

"Really? I thought I detected a Kiwi accent there—beneath a posh 'façade.' London and now Paris, oh my, isn't that *just* wonderful. Don't you just adore the French? Apart from their fearful cowardice in blowing up the *Rainbow Warrior*, of course. But never mind that, my dear." That grin again. "Come downstairs when you're ready, it's time for evening snacks. I've baked pavlova!"

She leaves me. I shut and lock the door out of reflex. I sit on the bed and almost bounce clear off it.

I think about pavlova. Emmanuelle had never eaten pavlova until she came here. She said it was like eating baby food, sweet fluffy baby food. "How can you say that?" I'd said. I'd actually defended the stuff, but only because she screwed her nose up at it. "You didn't even take a bite with the kiwifruit! You have to try that!" I'd made her try more, pushing the whipped cream and a slice of Kiwi into her mouth, but she spat it out, jumping up from the booth in that shitty cafe in Fox Glacier, "I said I don't like it!" she spat. "You're just a bully, Stephanie! *Pauvre connasse!*" she ran out onto the main road. Later she calmed down, we had that spa pool in our motel room, she liked that, she bounced on the spongy bed with me, we bounced so hard she had to cling to me to stay on.

Downstairs I tell Val I'm heading out for a quick dinner before everything shuts.

"Of course," she says, in a hurt tone, handing me a key to the front door.

"I'll pay you now? I have to leave at seven for the..."

"...whales." Val finishes. "I know. Don't you worry about a thing. Breakfast is served from six a.m. for that very purpose. I retire early to get up at five everyday except Christmas."

"That's grand."

I give her the one hundred and promise not to eat any dessert at the cafe; I'll save room for her pavlova.

"It'll be waiting for you on the counter!"

The teashop is still open. Talk Talk plays, 'It's a Shame' and for a second I am seventeen again, trying to seduce Juliet Castles (gorgeous, bronzed, but what a class-A bitch) and eventually succeeding, but dumped anyway by morning light and never spoken to again. I shudder, struggling out of my wet jacket with sudden fury. The room is full and there's only one young, blonde waitress. Even before I sit down I know the waitress is useless because everyone stares at her to get her attention, rather than talking to each other.

I order crayfish salad, fries, and a bottle of Sauvignon Blanc. I know it's too much wine to drink on my own, but for a second there I thought Emmanuelle was still with me. It's not far to drive back to Val's. I won't be leaving Kaikoura tonight and my body sags into this thought, not caring anymore. It's funny how you start down a path, not even sure it'll pan out, but then the thing you're aiming for materializes and it's a surprise. London's been like that. I thought I'd last two months there; it's been six years. I might not have all that much to show for it, yes, Emmanuelle, it's true I haven't bought a flat or even a car, but those things are just the trappings. I've got a life there. Just because everyone else is desperate to own shit, doesn't mean I am. I'm beyond that.

The waitress, no older than seventeen, brings the wine. She forgot the carafe of water. She realizes and says she'll be back. She brings the crayfish, forgets the fries, returns with the fries, opens the wine. Forgets the sauces. "I'm sorry," she apologizes, "I'm a really sucky waitress."

"Yes," I agree, "you sure are."

She looks like I just slapped her. I laugh to show I didn't

mean it in a bad way. She laughs along, flustered.

The sauce over the crayfish tastes like glue and the tomato is practically rancid, but the wine is cold and before I know it I've drunk it all.

Later, under Val's cacophonic floral bedcovers I can't sleep. The rain sluices down outside. Val's gutters need clearing— there's a sound like a whale pissing onto corrugated iron. I think about the last time with Emmanuelle, on twin beds as soft as these in another Bed & Breakfast, ending up her cheek against the textured wallpaper.

I wake up, sweating. It's the middle of the night, still raining. I'm thirsty after the wine. It's insane, a Bed & Breakfast, if you think about it. This is some woman's house. She lets any old person in. We could be anyone. I think about thirteen people killed on November 13th. That rampage in Rairumu. That shooting spree on Mount Ruapehu. I keep up with the news of murders here from London. I guess it's a hobby. I scan *The New Zealand Herald* online for any hint of homicide. I read and reread the details: a foreign couple found bludgeoned to death, a middle-aged Englishwoman raped and left to die by the side of the road, a man who shot his whole family on a Sunday morning except for the lucky 11-year-old granddaughter. I've mythologized my homeland, as all good Kiwis who leave do, but I've made it a place of violence and darkness.

I wonder if Val's sleeping badly tonight, her dreams invaded by visions of French assassins, *à la* Rainbow Warrior, here to blow up the boat heading out to see the whales, to blight Kaikoura's tourism and cause the senseless deaths of dozens of tourists, maybe even a whale mother and calf? Val, trusting Val, safe in bed with your cats, full of pavlova, how do you sleep knowing you could be shot, or have your head cut off by an axe, or be battered to death by a brick in a stocking?

I go to the shared bathroom on the landing. I drink water out of the tap. I pee and wash my hands. On the landing I pause. I hear noises from the room opposite. An argument, low and rapid, heated. Who are we sharing a house with? I saw nobody, coming in late, bypassing the pavlova. There could be murderers in that room, addicts who've heard that Val accepts cash only and they're about to go downstairs, grab her by a handful of her gray-blonde greasy hair, kick any cat that hisses in the head, and slowly garrote her as they whisper that her pavlova was really sucky and they're going to bleed her dry.

I creep downstairs, following the glowing water dispenser to the light left on in the kitchen. The pavlova has deflated somewhat, from being left out on the speckled gold Formica countertop. I take a big slotted spoon off a hook above the stove and eat half of it, stabbing the slices of kiwi and shoving them in quick so I hardly taste the mix of sweet and acid. I open cupboards, taking in the mountains of Tupperware in the pantry, stacked bottles of preserves, gingham tea towels folded a yard high, well-worn mismatched china with faded gold rims and scratched off daisy pattern. Tomorrow night's bread brews under a red gingham tea towel in a wooden bowl. The table is set for eight.

I move through to the back room, opening the door gently.

Val breathes heavily, curled child-like on one side of a double bed, a fat half-leg poking out for air, the other side of the bed occupied by two fat cats, alert, not purring, staring at me unblinking, they are used to strangers in the house but not strangers in this room, they're clueless as to how to react. "*Pauvre connasse,*" I whisper. Val shifts her wide ass in her sleep, nudging the cats, who stretch and settle down, closing their glowing eyes.

Her room is cluttered with heaped clothes either dirty or clean but musty-smelling all the same, a shabby claw-shredded armchair, lace doilies embroidered eons ago, portraits in frames of shadowy figures: the dead or gone husband, the dead or gone daughters. I move closer, easing myself into the armchair, breathing in a vague scent of gardenia and I close my eyes. I won't speak and wake her up; I will listen and not sleep, as I did in Queenstown, Milford Sound, Wanaka, Fox Glacier, Akaroa, and Christchurch. I will listen and wait for her to make the first move and then I'll jump up and say the perfect thing to calm her down. Say I'm there to protect her from the others, the freaks who are here under this roof with us, and she'll stop screaming in surprise and smile, and thank me.

At five, Val's alarm goes and the filter coffee starts brewing automatically and her homemade bran muffins, bread, and jams are all ready to be put on the table. The butter waits to be put out to soften up a touch more. The cats meow to be let out or fed. Upstairs, the guests take turns in the shared bathroom, moving quickly, not spending too long in the shower, aware that everyone needs their time, packing up so they'll be able to leave straight after breakfast, coming down in sleepy ones and twos until all are at the table, ready.

I am already miles north, and now the sun breaks through and the wind drops. The rain slows to a sweet mist. I pull over to see the gray coastline. Big and small oblong stones cover the beach like heads and fists.

Fur seals sunbathe out on nearby rocks. Emmanuelle taught me their name.

"*Phoques!*" It's pronounced 'fock.' The word cracks me up. "Phoques, phoques, phoques!"

I hurl the largest stones I can grab into the water, scaring the seals underwater, sweating in the sun. Eventually I drive on, to Blenheim.

Anon 2

I AM SITTING IN CAFÉ de Varenne waiting while Miriam has her daily tryst with Jesus Christ.

That's not his real name, but when Miriam told me about her affair with him, I kept saying, "Jesus Christ. Jesus Christ." As in, if this ever got out, it would be curtains. So I encrypt his name to JC for short.

JC is a politician. I've never voted for him. Miriam doesn't mention if she has either. She never mentions his work, or how she feels about it, to me. Of course, she talks to him about his work, but that's supposedly the point of meeting with him daily, Monday to Friday.

I don't overhear their pillow talk. I am their cover, their gooseberry.

Am I wrong to act this way? I collude, I bolster her fears and yet harpy on, subtly, but enough to show I disapprove. If I really disapproved, shouldn't I turn my back on the whole disgusting business? Cut her out of my "unsullied" life. I say to myself I'm being a true friend. But, I'm also living vicariously, sucking some morbid delight out of seeing beautiful Miriam collide with Fate, as I deep down believe she will, destroying her world with this nonsense? I must be a bad friend. I've slowed down, stopped the car even, to cradle the head of the car crash victim. Worse than rubber necking. I'm aiding and abetting. My hands are red.

Leonard and I come home clutching our stomachs. We ate too much again. There is moaning and Oxyboldine dissolved in a little Evian. The culprits were the Baileys, again. Rick and Miriam had a little soirée, only six of us, and the main course was *gésiers*, entrails and gizzards—it's like eating a bird's throat and dubious "second stomach," one should never eat throats for the main. As an entrée, a salad of gésiers is acceptable. But never as the main. My stomach is distended from too much wine, Leonard's from too much throat. We lie on the couch, our usual spot where we go to feel sorry for ourselves.

I started early on the wine. Café de Varenne had been a long wait and I was impatient, so I drank two kirs to make Miriam feel sorry for me waiting for her all afternoon while she was with JC. Then, Rick called and he wanted to invite a couple round to dinner that night, and Miriam said she was with me, so they should invite me and Leonard, and Rick said that sounded *wunderbar* and they agreed on 8.30.

I texted Leonard, who wrote back "COOL XXX," as is his habit. We aren't the kind of couple who use autotext shortcuts—those three Xs take time to tap in, you have to pause after each X, to allow the next X to surface, or else you end up with a lot of Ys and Zs. It's a comfort that Leonard keeps taking the time to send those three Xs, it means we are still in love.

I offered to help Miriam prepare, we blatted round to the fruit shop on rue de Sèvres, and she insisted on scouring the épicerie of Le Bon Marché, which houses numerous exotic goods that Miriam adores to waste money on. She has many complicated recipes that she invents. Two reds, a white from Nicolas. Lemons last minute. A tarte from the bakery around from their apartment. Our hands are heavy, weighed down, burdened with food wrapped in semi-translucent papers in blues, pinks, yellows. We dump everything on the kitchen counter and Miriam says, "No time for a lie down."

She's fibbing again, she's had a lie down with JC, of course, while I waited at the café, but I stay quiet, agree absently, saying it really is hard work throwing together a dinner and she's so good at it. "Rick's so lucky."

She pulls a face, "No, I'm lucky to have his love. Oh, I don't know what I'd do..."

Here's where Miriam, in tears, laments her deeds, prays for Rick's innocence of her evil deceit. She calls herself all sorts of names, ties herself in knots of morality and at the end of it all confesses she contemplates suicide daily. She is trapped, she tells me, by her love for both men.

Throughout all this, she's preparing dinner, and I sip from a glass of white wine. I poured Miriam a glass, but she won't touch it. I wait for my cue, when the tears slow. She's ripped a whole head of lettuce into pieces, chopped tomatoes savagely, nearly amputated her thumb, almost burnt the heel of her hand, herbs have been blitzed by the knife. Here's where I say:

"It'll all work out, don't feel bad. It's not your fault. It's JC who's been chasing you. You aren't going to stay with him, it's just temporary. This is just a momentary lapse."

I diagnose Miriam like her affair is a bout of the flu,

requiring two aspirin and a call in the morning. We eventually pass onto other topics. I've finished another two glasses and the kitchen is a maelstrom. Everywhere she touched is marred with peels, scraps, empty wrappings, spilt juices, debris. She doesn't clean up as she goes. She leaves the whole thing for her femme de ménage in the morning, who must almost collapse on arrival to this marvelous, huge kitchen that transforms into chaos every night, as if by monkeys, and every morning she must scrub, wipe down, put back into pristine order. It is her room of straw that she confronts with no smile. I've forgotten the woman's name. She is from Albania. She told me once that Albanians have traveled everywhere, they are the inveterate émigrés.

We drift into the lounge and Miriam freshens up her blush and lipstick. I color my lips, staring into the mirror above the mantelpiece. This room is large and I clash with the muted greens, raspberry, and cream silk velour. It's almost a sundae, mint and berry, while I wear my habitual black and look too hard to be admitted entry—with my skin the color of cold marble, my short hair in spiky blonde icicles, and my eyes like a frozen lake. You could skate over my eyes they're that hard. This is why I look good in black, but I don't suit Miriam's décor. She does. This room accentuates out her charming luck of being able to wear color. I sit severe and hard like marbles knocking into each other.

Miriam has startling green eyes. Nobody in the world has eyes like hers. I've heard her say at parties she is a quarter Irish, an eighth Jamaican, and three-eighths Spanish—which leaves a quarter unknown. Miriam has never mentioned what the other quarter of herself consists of; she acts as if her fractions add up to a whole, but they don't. I don't like to point this out. It would only upset her. But it upsets me that she won't admit that she leaves out the balance of the truth. Miriam tells the truth, but not the whole truth, and certainly not nothing but the truth. She's very convincing in this.

Her green eyes, then, are the focal point to her whole self, or three-quarters of self. Otherwise, her body is getting so model-like thin that she is in danger or wearing herself out. She used to have curves but now there's nothing. Miriam thinks this is fine and dandy, as the clothes she likes to wear look better with bone jutting out here and there. Her mix of race has left her with a perfect olive complexion, virtuous bone structure, and Dr Nebot has recently whitened her teeth so that her smile is as it was when she was fifteen, again. Blinding white and even; her teeth line up just so. I've asked her if she had orthodontic braces as a girl but she couldn't seem to remember.

Leonard and Rick look fine in any room. They've got the simplicity of what men wear, which inevitably doesn't require much thinking about. The couple who are turning up, well, we won't know how they fit in the room until it's too late. He is a business colleague that Rick is trying to impress, she is inconsequential. Miriam will turn on the charm to both and Leonard and I provide light entertainment. It's the usual drill.

As it turns out, when Rick arrives he's already met the couple outside the building and brought them up. Leonard will be ten minutes late, his norm. The couple shake off their coats and look around. The wife is someone I take an instant dislike to. She wears a cream turtleneck top that looks like Wolford. And a skirt with Wolford stockings. And carries a Burberry handbag. She's just too much already and I don't even know her name.

Rick Bailey is a nice guy. He towers over people, with the right mix of lank and paunch to have presence whilst remaining relatively lean. The French cuisine is starting to impact on his abdominals, a trial to Miriam who constantly nags him to go to the gym, go to the gym, as she goes to the gym. But, his belly gives him a humanity that he'd otherwise have lost. His face is somber, he frowns in worry, his glasses are slightly old fashioned, his hair grows too fast and he forgets to get a trim every four weeks as he should, it is shaggy again already, he's a puppy, really, but then he'll laugh and start to talk round the table and what comes out of his mouth is clever and unselfish, he gives people their soapbox and his commentary is never cutting, it is always generous and captivating.

I've never heard him bad mouth a soul, except that neighbor who died over summer in the heat wave. "His face turned navy," Miriam whispered, "Navy blue. Then he keeled right over. It was forty-three degrees. We left that night for Deauville."

Rick said stiffly, "He deserved it. When the SAMU came and took him away, him nearly capsizing the stretcher, I came up here and opened a bottle of champagne and celebrated."

I can't remember what the neighbor had done to incur this wrath, but it involved both of them and they felt deeply, personally, wounded. There was no last minute reconciliation.

So, Rick, who is turning thirty-three, the age of Jesus on the cross, introduces us to Anna and Philippe. I start drinking more steadily and Miriam passes around canapés of foie gras and Leonard ought to be here by now. Miriam and Anna have oodles in common, she lives in the sixteenth but that's acceptable to Miriam, who rather likes people to live in the sixteenth because that's all the fewer who are brave enough to live in the sixth, and Rick and Philippe have the world to conquer over there, chit chatting about the logistics. They'll be carving up everything just like Spain and Portugal did yonks ago. You take this half, I'll take the other, roger? And the doorbell rings, I go answer it myself, as that's allowable, I am practically family. Leonard and I kiss.

Halfway through the meal, when I've tried and tried to manage my throat—the disgusting gésiers salad, but have ingested only the vegetables that accompany it, and have nibbled the bread even though Miriam swears all women shouldn't eat the bread, nor the cakes, it adds kilos and kilos— I realize in a moment of clarity, that Miriam and Rick aren't talking to each other.

All evening, the boys have talked shop and the girls have talked shopping, épilation, interior decoration. I have been on the fence, tossing in a comment on either side from time to time, but I've just clicked that Rick didn't even kiss Miriam when he came in, and she has remained miles away from him.

After the ghastly food—the throats went down like a bomb, it was a mad idea that I should've forbidden Miriam to pursue—we have cigars and liqueurs around the coffee table. Rick finally has Miriam by his side. Her face is turned towards

Anna, playing the good hostess, but really ignoring Rick. He kneads her shoulder and has Philippe eating out of the heart of his hand. Leonard and I have accompanied the evening like a piquant sauce, adding just the right sort of social lubrication and I feel sick of everything. I've been out all day. I didn't intend for that. Tomorrow's the weekend, I never see Leonard all week and now I've gone and buggered up Saturday with the headache I'll have all morning. The liqueur burns going down. I squeeze Leonard's hand. Miriam yawns and everyone knows the night is over.

At home we lie on our couch, stomachs exploding, heads ringing.

"Did you notice a certain frostiness between Rick and Miriam?" I start.

"She's falling out of love with him. It won't last. I'll win the bet at this rate."

"We're wicked to make bets anyway."

"They're easy targets."

Leonard holds his stomach like a troubled toddler. I crawl into bed and we must sleep now.

Strangely, Miriam no longer needs hand-holding to make it to Café de Varenne and beyond. She assures me there's no difference, JC has seen to it that no alerts are necessary. He has taken an apartment, its whereabouts a secret to all, including me. Miriam goes directly there. She sometimes passes by his offices in her 'role' as decorator but it's not for the trysts. They have created a new space for that.

She and Rick arrive late for dinner at ours on Saturday. She
is flushed and gorgeous in a brown dress that other women
would wear badly. It might be Prada. The other guests rise to
greet her. Xander is a journalist, Bernard is a psychiatrist and
Larissa is writing her memoirs about various affairs she'd had.
None of their occupations faze Miriam. She is gracious and
intrigued by everyone. At one stage, between the salad leaves
and the cheeses, she follows me into the kitchen and whispers.

"I'm going to leave Rick."

"Stop it."

"I know," she giggled, "I'm kidding. But tonight I could've,
quite merrily, just disappeared. He is such a pain."

She leans against the kitchen counter as she says this. The
way her body drapes makes her limbs look out of proportion.
In her hand is the very nice Bordeaux we'll all been having
rather too much of, cradling the glass, her arm is twisted
around and the brown cap sleeve falls strangely, so it seems
she has no bicep and her arm is a doe's—thin and vulnerable.
She doesn't practice such poses in a mirror, this is all natural
Miriam. The vibrant victim. I give her arm a squeeze as I walk
past with more bread.

"You'll have to tell me later."

A look of suffering flashes over her—to be not listened to
by me!—but she follows me out. At the table she is happy as
Larry again, getting even cagey Bernard to open up about his
life. Everyone sits around her like gutted fish. She somehow
compels them to spill all. Larissa cries a little about her dead
father. Bernard's divorce is divulged. Xander admits he is

about to quit journalism and join the Peace Corps. I know nothing about these people (my supposed acquaintances, not hers), it is Miriam who flushes them out. They know nothing about her, in return. Rick laughs suddenly, for no real reason as if he's seen this trick countless times and it's still as amusing as ever, but his laugh has an edge of hysteria. He has drunk a lot with Leonard, who will drink to keep everyone company, not to escape but to empathize. I seem to drink out of a sort of fury.

Everyone moves onto the couches and by now Xander is completely in love with Miriam and she sits beside Rick, ignoring him, he clutches his balloon of Hennessy and she leans sideways to discuss the Peace Corps' inner intricacies with her new-found buddy. I can just tell that tomorrow she will express a lifelong secret desire to volunteer for the Peace Corps and run away to China. That she just this minute remembered. This new fascination will last about a week, until Anna or another bourgeois pal gets her hooked on the latest peel, scrub, tonification, diet regime, or exercise trend. In the past six months alone, she's been into Pilates, shiatsu massage, Cellu-6 body jiggling to combat cellulite (at the local beautician's), sent away a strand of hair for DNA testing to find out what diet to stick to, been a slave to Eat for your Blood Type (she's O, it was easy for her), drunk that Easi-Diet garbage, been on protein bars flavored Caramel, Vanilla, Berry, joined a Badminton club, quit coffee, quit carbs, quit dairy, quit cigarettes, signed up for hydrotherapy classes, seen a top nutritionist who works for the Bolshoi Ballet Company, been to her osteopath who cricks her bones back into alignment (a God she swears by), run seven miles per day, had Coaching for her weights program, had a chemical peel, a spot of Botox, drunk three liters of water per day, and tried a new facial steaming program every other week. Miriam epitomizes the French 'health' system, seek and seek and never stick to one solution. Try it all.

I kiss all cheeks goodnight and flop onto the couch for another digestif and the dinner dissection with Leonard.

"Well, I admit they were all eating out of Miriam's hand there. It's so sad seeing grown adults cry and moan on like that."

"And Rick!"

"And Rick," Leonard agrees.

It is rather bad of us, all this, but it's fun. I don't see it as feeding off of others' misery, because I don't see these people as miserable. They are all happy, happy, happy. They just don't see themselves. Does anyone?

Weeks pass. Miriam doesn't tell me where she goes now, to meet JC, or even if she is still decorating his offices. She can't have the time for it. I am annoyed with Miriam for continuing this, and for not doing something about Rick.

And then she goes and does something.

"Hi darling, I've left Rick. It's over," Miriam sounds flat, black and white to the extremes, there is no gray left now, "Can you come visit? I've moved into the apartment."

"What apartment?" I ask, even though it must be the one JC set up. I just want her to admit that.

"It's on rue de Rivoli, overlooking Tuileries, the entrance is off Saint Honoré. Can you come over?"

"Is that the love pad then?"

"Listen, if you're going to be sarcastic, then just forget it. I'm feeling really bad about all this and if you're not going to support me as a friend, then I can't see you at all. This is really hard."

She says all this sounding near tears. I submit, soothe her feathers, promise to pop round straight away. I take down the numbers of the address. I decide to walk there. It's on my side, the Right Bank. Funny, I never thought Miriam belonged on this side. She'll be overlooking the Louvre where Marie Antoinette was kept in confinement, the vast Louvre as a pretty prison, until she was beheaded in Place de la Concorde.

She is indeed overlooking the Louvre. And Jardin des Tuileries. She can stretch her neck and see up Concorde and the Champs. She can practically pick out her favorite haunts on the Left Bank. I ruminate over which orange chimney pot was her and Rick's. Her apartment, or JC's apartment (or the Government's even) is airy but badly decorated. It has been ripped out of a page of *Elle Décor* from the mid-eighties, all glass and mirror and black with carpet in a nasty cream that has seen parties, had heels pricked into it, had Dom Pérignon spilt over it, had cashews crushed into it. The carpet is world-weary with the débâcles it has suffered. The bedroom is garish. No wonder Miriam is holding back the tears.

"Is JC letting you gut it?" is the first thing I ask.

She makes us a pot of herbal tea and brings it out of the coin cuisine, which is too tiny to ever cook for more than two people. Which is the point. There'll be no dinner parties here.

"I mean, the view is amazing, but are you able to rip up the carpet?"

She bristles, "I'm able to do anything I want. This is my apartment."

"Sure," I agree, "but didn't JC—find it for you?"

This she keeps refusing to answer. I want to demand to see the title deed on the place. She insists it's just something she's picked up and is now in sole possession of, without giving a single detail to substantiate how and when this occurred. It is absolute bullshit. She must've been told to stop referring to her liaison with JC. Deny, deny, deny. It's rather boring, sitting in this apartment. The sun streams in, the Eiffel and the Seine twinkle in the distance, but it's all dead inside. The air is cooped up.

"You have minor decorating plans then?"

This is suddenly a safe topic now I've dropped the mention of JC. She launches, "Oh sure. I'll repaint and change some of the furniture. The layout is wonderful. There's a dressing and salle de bain off the bedroom. And a guest toilet by the door. This living space is great."

For one person to occupy. And one visitor. You couldn't have socially acceptable parties in here. The parties this carpet has suffered—they must've been orgies.

"Can we open a window?" I ask finally.

"Oh no," Miriam frowns. "The windows don't. I'll turn up the air-con if you like, it's built in."

So this is like Marie Antoinette's Louvre. The eighth floor, top curved space of the building, all glittering silver roof and glass from the outside, a glass cage from the inside with that horrible cream on the floor muffling any objections. I decide it might be better to meet Miriam out in future. A tea salon, or God, please a wine bar. I kiss near to her cheeks and left.

We see Rick, and he's not himself. He drags his fingers through his hair and talks about taking up with various women they've had over for dinner who he never laid a finger on previously. He just might take up with one, or even two of them. That'll bring Miriam running.

When questioned, carefully, as if he may implode if we push too hard, we tease out the scene of departure. It was a Sunday morning and Rick had a hangover. Miriam dressed and told him she was leaving him for awhile. She left most of her things, just packed one bag and said, "I'll send for my things."

"What do you mean you're leaving? How long for?"

Miriam pursed her lips and said, "I'll let you know."

It was open-ended. Not burning her bridges. In case. He assumed she was shacked up with a lover.

"Probably on Ile-St-Louis, the fucking cow," he bowed his head and wiped his face furiously. Angry at himself for feeling.

For Christmas, Miriam invites her pals out to dinner and we all rock along in ankle length frocks to a private dining room at the Crillon no less. Personally I would've thought she'd go for something less stuffy, more fun. But this is not "fun Miriam," this is Miriam deigning. She's invited that Anna and Philippe who she's somehow gained custody of in the split-up with Rick. Anna is as vacuous as ever and Philippe talks to Leonard amiably enough but later I'm sure Leonard will tell me he had nothing interesting to say. Along with them are *my* friends Xander, Larissa, and what's-his-name. Not an attaché of JC's in sight. No evidence of the man except around Miriam's neck and wrist, in lines of white gold with tiny diamonds studding her like a branded animal. Her fingers are barren. She's abandoned her wedding ring, engagement ring and the others gifted from Rick, or bought herself. Her bare hands look sullen, in fact, as if they are waiting for a new set of rings, from JC, and are sulking that the goodies haven't been delivered yet.

"Wherever did you find Xander et al?" I ask her in the ladies.

"Oh, we've kept in touch is all, he called me the other week so I said why not come along? He's the one who suggested bringing Larissa. And Bernard rings me from time to time also."

Strange, since she has a new mobile number (to avoid Rick's little chats that always end in liquid recriminations). Funny that Xander and Bernard guessed her new number— that they ring her and not vice versa. But then, I don't want to point out the flaws in her logic, she'll only get peevish.

Miriam looks round and round the table, her eyes large as saucers, lips parted as she murmurs small encouragements to all around her, that yes, we should keep yapping away, chatting about fuck-all, sharing banalities, that that was just how she wanted things. That this was successful, as far as dinner parties go. It was awful though, we all should've been round Rick and Miriam's enormous coffee table, causing a pigsty for the Albanian lady who is no doubt having to clear away Rick's Speed Rabbit Pizza boxes and empties of Heineken and ashtrays full, every morning.

Miriam has been testing all of us. If we complain that management is doing a lousy job, that's a jibe at her, and therefore we are criticizing her and if that happens, it's like a bomb going off. Things will be shouted. Reactions will be overplayed. She will refuse to play nice. So it's best at the moment to keep mum. Say zip. I listened when she tore her heart out all over the kitchen floor, wept like a willow, and called upon Greek gods to smite her for her despicable behavior that made a mockery of Rick, of JC, of herself. She hated herself two months ago. She wanted to die, she said. She considered suicide, she told me. And every time, I had to flip faces, do a demi-tour and suddenly bolster. I realize, sitting here in the Crillon's Salon des Anges that if you don't constantly bolster, Miriam cuts you out of her life, out of her emotions, and you are set adrift on an iceberg and find yourself waving to the ship as it suddenly picks up speed and sails away.

I'm eating pigeon now—the too-rich sauce sticks in my throat—but really I'm waving to a speck on the horizon. Miriam has no further need. And I owe Leonard five euros since I naively, stupidly, bet that she and Rick *would* last way beyond spring.

Girls & Mothers

Faye 1

IT IS HIGH SUMMER. 1977. You're in the kitchen, painted optimistic Gregg's custard yellow, but on the wrong side of the house and *cold*, even today when it's broiling.

You chop up onion while butter sizzles. Throw in some thyme. Looking inside this dead chook makes you queasy.

The kitchen window overlooks the swing-set and weeping willow. You can't see the Fiberglass swimming pool, built on the other side of the yard to catch the sun, but Will's watching the three little kids—he's great at playing with them—a fifteen-year-old God of Fun. You hear them whooping and hollering. The two girls will be jumping in and out, in and out, orange armbands on, legs going high speed. The youngest, Leo, will stick to Will like a shadow, avoiding the water.

Leo can't swim. He'll learn when he's four.

The oldest three are at summer jobs down at the lake. They'll all come in wanting filling up. You hear one of the girls cry out, high-pitched, "I'm telling Mum!" Skye.

She treks wetly into the kitchen, streaming rivulets. Your shoulders tense.

"Ingwid's bein' mean!"

"What happened?"

"Ingwid says I don't say Wotowua wight and they won't let me go to school if I don't speak wight."

Skye can't pronounce the letter 'R.' The roof of her mouth is extremely high. Almost a cleft palate.

"Did you know Rotorua is a Maori name? It means 'second lake.' Roto means 'lake' and Rua means 'two.' Try saying it like this: Rrrrrotorrrrrua…"

Skye half listens, wiggling out an impromptu ballet dance.

"Do you need to pee?"

"No!" she hollers. The water running off her has created the perfect amount of glide on the lino. You like teaching your kids the names of things. You think it's equipping them for life. You learn local history and Maori words from chatting to the women at the Plunket Centre where you go for a cup of tea and the children's check-ups. You also learned Roto could mean 'inside' and Rua 'hole.' A reference to the geysers, the bubbling holes that erupt with scalding mud. As regular as clockwork or children's stomachs.

"Try it, Skye, use your tongue to make the Rrrrr sound."

Skye purses her lips. Her pink tongue works over the sounds but all that erupts is: "Wuuu."

"Never mind Ingrid. Go back and swim. Or you can tidy up the toys in the sunroom."

You continue stirring so every bit of bread gets a lick of butter. The trick is to give kids a choice out of two things: one that you want them to do and the other that they don't want to do. That keeps them happy, thinking they have the world going their way.

"No!!! I wanna stay in the pool."

"All right."

Skye skids out, victorious. She loses her footing and plunges headfirst towards the cabinet corner—catching herself before impact with Formica. Your shoulders relax.

Your fingers are coated with butter and flecks of sage. Bay leaves disappear into the carcass along with half a lemon. The juice finds nicks to fill with sting. For a while now, you've realized that your life consists of a series of movements of Chance. Everything's in a line of causality like dominoes. Like Skye, almost smashing into the sharp corner, but not. None of this is in your power to control. It's a horrible truth you've been avoiding. (This is a brainstorm. Not the coming-up-with-good-ideas kind of brainstorm, but a hurdy-gurdy cacophony of a mind that can't STOP.)

You rinse off the lemon juice and take up the needle and black thread. Take the *Titanic*. If your grandfather had used those tickets to emigrate, then Mummy would've surely died and you'd never have been born. Jack Norwood worked for Harland & Wolff in Belfast, as a cabinetmaker, and was offered free passage in steerage on the *Titanic's* maiden voyage. Jack told Adele to pack—they were moving to New York! His youngest girl—your mother—was six. But a day before the launch, Jack had second thoughts. The shipyard workers knew there were always hiccups—niggling things to be ironed out after the maiden voyage—and they'd never built a steamer as gigantic as this one. Jack decided to go on the second trip.

Take your uncle's party. Mummy immigrated to Canada at twenty-one, met Daddy and had you. Daddy worked at Domtar in Cornwall, Ontario, the big pulp-and-paper mill.

With the Depression, they started letting everyone go. Daddy was one of the last. They gave him rail tickets for your family to go anywhere in Canada, plus $400. Uncle Jerry threw a farewell party—you were heading out West where there was still work on farms, food to eat. But at the party, Daddy's wallet was stolen from his jacket lying on the bed. The tickets and money were gone. Daddy wanted to call the police, but Uncle Jerry wouldn't let him. So you stayed in Cornwall and Daddy returned to Domtar, but no longer as a manager, on the floor of Bleaching—his lungs turned to rice paper from the chlorine. Nobody in Bleaching lived past fifty-five. You fished pike and perch from the Saint Laurence to eat. He took you out once, but you threw a fish back when Daddy turned to light his pipe, feeling the slippery life wriggle out of your hands. That made him mad as hops. "That was our dinner!"

The chicken looks better once he's sewn up. You don't like to look at the insides of things. Raw holes where something ought to be.

Your spirits flag listening to Skye outside, "Ingwid!!! Give it to me—it's my tuwn!"

Was there enough for them all?

You start peeling the mound of potatoes. And if you hadn't read that book would you have immigrated to New Zealand? It was *Where the People Sing* about the Maori tribes of the Wairarapas, borrowed from the Community Library in Nepean. You felt muffled by the weather in Ottawa by then. The wind left you defenseless. In 1960, Diefenbaker harped on about the Bomb and cranked up his Oscrek Drill—it was always *when* the Bomb dropped, not *if*. Duck and cover. Radio

Two made jingles out of people's fears. Nuclear testing happened in the Nevada desert, Siberia, the northern Pacific. To stay in the Northern Hemisphere meant fallout. Fathers built bomb shelters in their basements. Radio programs debated whether it was ethical to shoot people who tried to break into your shelter, or if it was acceptable to shut neighbors out because, after all, you'd only have enough provisions for you and your family. Dogs and Mr. & Mrs. Nice could, in good conscience, be left outside to die of radiation poisoning. Not shot, just left outside.

You and Richard didn't build a shelter. You moved to New Zealand.

The potatoes are on to boil now. It's Leo's birthday today and his favorite—banana cake—cools on the rack. Well, you say it's his favorite. It's the only cake you know off by heart, so it's become the favorite. You hear the girls shrieking and Will trying to calm them down. He's a good boy to take care of those three like he does. There's time to do the icing.

When you told Richard about the interesting people of the Wairarapas from that book, he said, "For two pins I'd move there!" And you said, "Here's two pins, let's go." It was as if you and Richard kept... what? Daring each other...? To move, have another child, change job, house, or town. Because to stay put might mean... what? Mortality? Giving into Chance?

So you sold your house, gave the dog to Mr. & Mrs. Nice, packed up fifty boxes, took the train out West and boarded the P&O liner *Orcades* bound for New Zealand. That first winter was touch-and-go. The chill got inside your mind in a way

like a hedgehog, sinking lower, hands moving the water around him uselessly. Blue eyes bulging as they lock onto yours. A bubble from his mouth. You fight through the water. Is this up to Chance? Your arms are strong, pushing the water away and you grab Leo and shoot you both to the surface.

Will is taking off his tee shirt, preparing to dive into rescue. The girls are frozen.

Leo's arms are limp—not hugging. Will helps roll him onto the deck as you climb out. Your clothes cling and you want to shake everything off—the last ten minutes—every piece of the past that's stuck on you. Scatter the dominoes. Leo's white tee shirt wraps him like a shroud. You drop and blow short puffs into his mouth and nose. Skye makes ragged yelps.

"Dial 0 for operator, Will," you gasp. "Ambulance."

You hear unreal fear in your voice.

You pump Leo's chest, your fingers claw at his neck for a pulse. His lips are light blue. Your hands slip with a residue of butter. You blow another four breaths into his lungs. Desperate fingers press at his neck. At his wrists. Is that something? That? Water runs off you. Your fingers can't keep hold of these veins, as slippery as fish.

Everything is slipping beyond your grasp.

"They said in a jiffy, Mum." Will squats to squeeze Leo's hand. "Come on, come on."

You left them too long.

"Take the girls inside."

You pump at Leo's chest. Blow in air. When you moved to Rotorua, Doctor Doyle took the time to listen and instead of prescribing Valium again, he gave you a blessing.

"You're almost thirty-nine," he said, "but the likelihood of Down's syndrome isn't significant what with your previous healthy pregnancies. You could have more, if you want to." And you remember how light you felt walking home? You told Richard, and that's how you had these perfect beings: Ingrid, Skye, and Leo.

Leo splutters and water geysers out of his blue lips. A sob bubbles from inside, and you hug him tight. His chubby hand reaches for your sleeve and pats the swirling colors. You stay with him on the smooth wooden deck, stroking his cheek.

The air is so warm and calm it hums.

Skye 1

I WAS ALL BY MYSELF and getting sick of stabbing jellyfish with a stick and throwing the bits into the sea. The sun came in and out of clouds, but the wind was warm. There was only the water licking the sand and the sounds of generators purring like cats behind our shop. A broken Fanta can and newspaper wrappers from somebody's fish and chips sat on the beach. I picked them up with the tip of my stick and threw them in the dusty bin on the roadside. I was about to go back home and walk along our concrete wall that reads: 'Mulberry Grove Store' except then a man and a lady came walking off the beach from the stream end. They held hands. Plus they had sunglasses on their heads. A black camera hung around his chest like a third eye.

"Come on, Rick," the lady said, "maybe up that road."

"Aw, I don't know, DeeDee."

They sounded like *The Six Million Dollar Man* and *The Bionic Woman* (which is seven o'clock Thursday night, and half past six Wednesday night, TV Two. All my favorites are on TV Two). The man kicked a lump of wet sand that fell apart after one push. She dragged him towards Rosalie Bay Road up behind our shop.

I started to follow them, with my stick that was still wet

from a last jellyfish's insides. We passed Ivan and Gladys' motel where the family with the children called Troy and Tiffany come every summer and we all play on the motel trampoline. The man started pulling the lady towards the motel, but she shook his hand off and stood, playing with her hair, sticking the long blonde ends into her mouth. Mum said never do that or you end up with a big hairball in your stomach and then you can die. Then they saw me.

I scratched my leg with my stick. They studied my mousey hair hanging over my purple-rimmed glasses, hiding my eyes, my scruffy tee shirt and shorts and my mismatched jandals because I've already lost three this summer in Lost Jandal Creek.

"Welcome," I said with a little bow. To show them I'm not scared of strangers. That all tourists were welcome on the island, they were money to Mum and Dad, working in the shop. I pretended to be Tattoo on *Fantasy Island* (which is eight o'clock Friday night, TV Two).

"Hey there, can you tell us, there any special attractions to see over that hill?" the man asked.

I wondered what was "special attractions."

His dark hair stuck in curls around his neck and he wiped his hand on his white shorts. Now the lady shifted from leg to leg as if her feet hurt. I shrugged.

"Maybe, I don't think so."

Rosalie Bay Road led to the other side of the island. I didn't know of anything over there. I played in every other direction but this one. I'd never gone further than where we were standing. But I didn't want to say that.

"See our swings? Mr. Todd made them for us, and the flying fox and the see-saw. The big swing goes right out over this road. Really high."

"Who's Mr. Todd?" The man crouched down like I was a baby. I twirled my stick around like a baton to show I was a big girl, not a baby. He straightened up when the stick got too close to his camera.

"Mr. Todd has lived here on the island forever. He's one hundred years old."

Mr. Todd liked to push us kids on the swings, but one time I saw him push Suzie-May so high that everyone could see her undies so that's why I never wear skirts anymore when we play on the big swing or the flying fox. I don't want Mr. Todd to giggle like he did when everyone saw Suzie-May's undies. I don't know what my undies would look like from down low.

The man looked bored. The lady sucked on pieces of her long blonde hair.

I told them all about how Charline O'Sullivan had broken her arm a few weeks earlier on that very swing and how Ingrid (that's my sister) and I ran and ran to the shop, completely puffed and got Mum to call the mainland for the ambulance plane to fly over and take Charline to the hospital. In Auckland. And how loud she screamed.

"She screamed her head off. That's an expression."

They nodded like all that was pretty special.

The man said, "So there's nothing else around here? Nothing special?"

I guessed my story wasn't special, after all.

"Come on, Rick," the lady DeeDee said, "She's a kid, not a

tour guide."

"Well, there's no guidebooks, are there? Not a word's written down about this god-forsaken island."

I didn't know what to say. They obviously didn't think much of our swings and the way you had to climb very high to get to that flying fox and how fast it went. How you sat on a small wooden bar that was very smooth and that Mr. Todd had carved himself, and how you flew down to land on the planks he'd built in the big tree at the end. These things weren't special enough for them. The lady shifted again from one foot to the other. The ends of her hair hung beside her tanned face, soaking wet from her sucking. Now I didn't want to tell this lady about how sucking your hair can maybe make you die.

I was going to leave them and run up the secret bush tracks to play something else, but then I saw Mr. Todd walking down the hill towards us. He was maybe more than 100 years old, his face had squiggles all over it, his hair was all white and his eyes were deep inside his face. He had hands like pohutakawa roots and always wore the same black jumper and gumboots with holey blue dungarees. He saw me from way up Rosalie Bay Road and he waved down. He must have good eyesight, not like me. I have very poor eyesight, which means that without my glasses the world is all a blur with no shape to anything. Today he carried a bucket to put pipis in from the beach and a long, smooth stick, like mine, but bigger and not as white.

"Mr. Todd," I pointed at the man and the lady, "These tourists want to see something special around here."

"Something special, eh? Well, I don't know," he wheezed and smiled. "Follow up this way."

He took us for a walk up Rosalie Bay Road, up past the farthest part I'd ever been on, up over the hill and then right, off the road, onto a track through cutty grass up a yellow mountain.

I walked behind the Tourists, trailing my stick. I never liked to leave a good stick and this one was smooth and light. Mr. Todd chatted away to the man, but the lady didn't say much. I heard funny big words: "sabbatical" and "thesis" and "anthropology." I repeated the words to remember them so I could ask Dad later, but the sun drilled into my head and I had to wipe my hair off my face all the time. I kept my eyes on the track. The cutty grass tried to catch my legs and rip me. I beat it back with my stick. The lady hung off the man's hand, but when the track got too narrow she had to walk behind him. Mr. Todd sang into the breeze. A Maori song that I knew from school but didn't know what all the words meant. I heard the man ask what it was called, but I couldn't hear Mr. Todd's low voice. He cackled at his own jokes, like the witch in Sleeping Beauty, which is on *The Wonderful World of Walt Disney* at six o'clock on Sunday night, right at teatime so we have to watch from the dinner table, straining to see the television around each other's big fat heads.

We came to a cave. It was narrow, only one-and-a-half-people wide and cut right into the middle of the mountain. Ferns grew around the mouth and gray planks made a doorway with a metal padlock that Mr. Todd unlocked. With the bush all around us, the cave was almost invisible. I had never seen a cave like this one before. We kids ran around all the bush tracks from Mulberry Grove down to Shoal Bay and the wharf where the barge comes in, and right the other way to Stonewall and Pa Beach, but I never saw any cave like this. Mr. Todd talked to the Tourists for a while but I didn't catch it all. I was using my stick to cut my name into the soft dark ground. S-K-Y-E. Maybe he asked them for money. I would of, if I'd known about this cave. I stared into the mouth. A cold smell came out from the insides. Like dug-up earth with maybe wetas in it and squirmy things you find when you lift a big rock. I could smell the tight fronds of the pungas. Tapu. It smelled tapu and I didn't want to go in there. But I had three adults around me. And then the Tourists looked at me, waiting, like they wouldn't go in there without *me*.

Mr. Todd said finally, "Come on, follow after." He walked inside holding up a torch he fished out of his jumper somehow. I started in second, with the Tourists last.

Shelves were carved into both walls from the ceiling right down to the ground, left and right. It was so narrow I could've reached out and touched both sides. Which I didn't. I didn't touch a single thing. I understood now. This *was* tapu. I hoped it must be okay, if Mr. Todd invited me in. He looked maybe a bit Maori. It must be his cave, so it's okay, I thought, I won't be cursed. I wasn't sure for the Tourists though, maybe he'd done it on purpose, lured them in here to curse them. He wouldn't want to curse me. I was only six. He liked us kids. Lots. He was always hanging around the playground to try and push us on the swings. He also hid chocolate bars for us under the wooden benches cut into the earth along the bush tracks. Cadbury's Dairy Milk chocolate. Bars of Milky Way. Peanut Slabs. Flakes.

Now, Mr. Todd pointed to the shelves, talking slow as a snake charmer: "That one's a horse femur. This one's a cat's skull. I've got a whole pelican here." On all the shelves were rows of bones. Cow bones, dog bones, wild pig tusks, Barrier rat bones as big as half-grown cats.

There were tiny mouse bones. Perfect and pale in the torchlight. The Tourists' bodies blocked most of the light but I squinted and made out a little skull and body sitting on a bed of dried fern. I moved very carefully behind Mr. Todd who held his torch up, swinging it from side to side, telling us all about his bones. We were almost at the end now. I wondered if anybody would notice I'd been gone for ages. At the end of the cave, the space widened to show, on the left and right, two full skeletons dangling from fencing wire. People bones.

"That one's a Maori. And this one's Pakeha. White man," he explained to the Tourists. The Maori man had a dent above where his ear should be. But there were no ears. Or nose. A wisp of something like hair stuck to his head. They both had tiny bones where their pee-pee sticks should've been. Their fingers were like many pieces of chalk. Fishing line and wire held them all together. Their bones were the same not-white color and the two skeletons faced each other at the end of the cave with big holes where the eyes go on real people and no smiles because they had no more lips. I felt very sad for them stuck in one place like that.

I wanted to ask Mr. Todd if he'd made this cave or found it, but I was scared that if he'd found it then it wasn't his to invite me into and I *would* be cursed because it was so tapu. I could smell it. The cold below crept up through my rubber jandals. The hairs on my shins stood up. I held my stick straight by my side. Not touching a thing. I was making sure I touched nothing, but I worried about my feet because they touched the floor. I hoped my jandals were enough of a barrier to protect me from the curse. My hair was in my eyes again but I didn't dare brush it away because I didn't want to lift my arm in case it touched something. I turned my head a little, to see sunshine past the Tourists and the green of the ferns at the mouth. I was all cold and stiff now, barely moving. I breathed in only spoonfuls of this cave air. The man had his camera out and I thought, "No, don't take a photo!" too late, as his flash went off like his 'oohs' and 'aahs' over the people bones. He squeezed past me to get closer. I made myself as flat as I could and sucked myself into nothing so he went past without pushing me against the shelves. His fingers reached out, towards the Maori skull with the dent and the bits of hair, but Mr. Todd's torch knocked them away.

"Better not touch. Been here a long time."

That's when I knew. Mr. Todd hadn't made this cave, he found it. *It wasn't his.* Or maybe it was his parents' cave, but still we *shouldn't* be in there. I really wanted out, I could hardly breathe. A long time might be two hundred years.

"Excuse me, Mr. Todd? Did you make this place?" The lady's voice had gone all drawn out and high like Daisy Duke but I couldn't even think of what time and what night *The Dukes of Hazzard* was on now, I was so scared. My stick jumped out of my hand and knocked against the shelves with the opossum bones. It fell onto the ground. I didn't want it now. Mr. Todd laughed like the lady made a joke. He came close to me, picked up my stick and handed it to me. He winked. I slowly took the stick from his ropey hands. I let out all the air inside me because his wink said, "Let's play a game with the Tourists." I knew he didn't want to curse me. I was one of his favorite kids. He always pushed me really high on the big swing with his hands going round my waist to start me off from very high. And now his arm slung over my shoulder. Cool and raspy where his old skin touched my arm. He hugged me to his leg and chuckled. His warm smell filled my nose: musky and a bit sour and tangy like if you bite silver foil and it makes you shiver. His torch flickered off then back on. Mr. Todd whacked it hard against his other leg. It stayed on, shining at a cat skeleton crouched on the shelf before me.

The man spoke, "Did you find it then?" He voice boomed in the cave and his eyebrows came together.

"I put this collection together. It's like a museum. I'm the caretaker."

The lady's hands flew out and gripped the shelf edges. She maybe thought he'd killed the people for their bones, but worse, she'd be cursed now for touching, I was sure of that. Even if Mr. Todd was the caretaker. Because the lady wasn't his favorite girl. I was. That made me safe. Not them. "Come on, Rick. We shouldn't be in this crypt. God." She looked sick, and all white. Whiter than the mouse bones.

She moved back to the mouth and we followed outside into the sunshine with Mr. Todd's hand guiding me, pressed into the middle of my back. I smiled at Mr. Todd and took off down the path with my stick. Flying past the cutty grass, nothing touching me. Knowing I'd never tell anyone about the bone cave because that would keep me double safe.

And I never saw those Tourists again.

Skye 2

"STOP IT NOW, LEO!"

"I'm not doing anything!"

"Ingrid, make him stop it!" I howl. Leo, who is five and ruining my life, brushes his teeth and dribbles toothpaste spit near my arm. The sink is lined with thick trails of white frothy drool.

Ingrid brushes her hair and ignores us.

Leo and I start shoving each other. He is two years younger, but with a layer of puppy fat insulating him from my pinches and slaps. He weighs the same as me now. It's getting harder to beat him up.

Ingrid says, "Hurry up, we're going to be late."

I push Leo off his wooden step that helps him reach the taps. He screams like he is being boiled alive. Will runs up the stairs.

"Now come on, you kids. Get your schoolbags. You've got to go. Leo, you're all right. Who pushed him?"

I say nothing.

Ingrid says, "Skye did."

"Well, that's enough. Skye, say sorry."

I mumble. We grab our schoolbags and clatter downstairs, through the shop, waving good-bye to our parents and cross the dirt road to walk along the beach to school.

Ingrid says it's a fifty meter walk. But I don't know what that means; to me, it's a sprint so that I'm not too puffed, or it's far enough to find about three good shells on the beach, or it's short enough to avoid a fight with Ingrid or Leo.

The Mulberry Grove School grounds are all ours. Before and between classes, whatever the latest game is, we run to get play time in before Mr. Fuller rings the bell to get inside. We play marbles, knuckle-bones, elastics, or sometimes the girls peel off for Sindys, paper dolls, hopscotch or four-square; and the boys start tag, blind man's bluff or war. Other times, the whole school rucks in for bulrush, kick the bucket or huts. Playtime and lunch disappear. There are never any arguments about exactly what point in the game we left on. Nobody starts each craze, they begin like waves: there's a down turn in enjoyment or a tiredness that spreads without words to tell us it's time to change the game. There are no fights and no winners.

Inside, between play, we learn things from the Fullers. There are only two teachers at the school. Mrs. Fuller teaches the Little Room and Mr. Fuller does the Big Room. After Mulberry Grove, we will have to do high school by correspondence or go to an Auckland boarding school off the island on the mainland. I moved up into the Big Room at the beginning of this year with my classmates. But then that little rat bag, Leo started school and cried all day everyday until Mr. Fuller talked to our parents and they all made me stay in the Little Room to soothe Leo. Mrs. F's bright red hair flames around Little Room like a bush fire. A natural disaster. Leo is scared of school, he still can't read, he only draws: big red dragons spewing sulfur in crooked crayon on brown waxed paper. Mrs. F stares at my painting during Art and sighs heavily.

"That is not a horse, Skye."

She takes my brush and squishes it into the brown color I made by myself and starts slashing the thin paper.

"*This* is a horse."

Once she's finished painting over my picture she carries on around the room. She always stops at her son's easel, "That's wonderful, Sebastian!"

Sebastian is a year younger than Leo but we've all been told he's gifted. He wears perfectly clean clothes everyday. But he doesn't join in all the games with us. He's allowed to play dolls, but his parents won't let him do bulrush ever since Jake Dallovich broke his arm. Today, it's huts, which is considered too rough, so Sebastian stays inside the classroom all lunchtime with Mrs. F bending over him. Making him learn to be gifted, I'll bet.

We three kids love lunch because Will comes down to school with the lunch orders. We always get lunch ordered, because it's our shop and Mum doesn't ever have time to make us lunch anyway. Ingrid and I order apple pie or filled roll or tuna fish sandwiches. Leo usually gets a mince pie. That's why he's got the puppy layer, plus because he sneaks behind the counter as soon as we get home to steal lollies from out of the boxes. All the other kids say hi to Will and he says hi to the older ones and gives us our lunch first. Then we all watch him sprint back down to the shop, his strong sixteen-year-old legs chewing up the grass. He's doing correspondence. He let us watch him dissect a mouse for Biology. It had lines of blue and red all through its insides. I was almost sick.

After lunch, our limbs are sore and warm from playing huts all hour, where my team was captured and tortured with Chinese burns on our arms given out by Ingrid, Mrs. F tells us we are having a school assembly.

We troop into the Big Room, I say hi to my classmates that I can't sit beside because of Leo. Ingrid ignores me. We look up at Mr. F, who stands at the front of the class, not smiling. Sebastian says, "Pick me up, Daddy!"

He clears his throat. Mr. F has dark, normal hair. He wears short sleeved shirts with a white singlet outlined beneath and checkered shorts to just above the knee. He sends me strict pages of exercises on Social Science and Mathematics so that I keep up with the Big Room's work. He marks my answers with a thick, red ball point pen. We are only allowed pencil until Form One which is three years away. Forever.

"We're all going on a field exercise this afternoon, so put away your books."

Everyone rustles with excitement. The older kids shove their books into their desks, letting the wooden tops bang shut. For the last field exercise, we sat on the four-square outline and waited until Mr. F said it was safe to look at the sun. He said if we peeked, we would go blind. Nobody peeked. We stared at ants crossing the white painted concrete. "You can look now, children," Mr. F pronounced. The sun was a total circle of pitch black. The school building, playing field and beyond, even our shop with our house on top of it, were all dark. But not a night dark. I could still make everything out. It was a nasty darkness. Not like when we have the flashlight shining through our hands and everything is red.

We are scared of field exercises.

"We're going to have a Tsunami Drill," Mr. F says. "Does anyone know what a tsunami is?"

I look around. Someone has to know. Karen White puts up her hand. She is in Form Two, next year she'll be going off the island or doing correspondence.

"A tidal wave?"

"Yes."

I know about those. Ingrid, Leo and I have been to the movie house eight times this year. Every time it's the same movie being shown by the man who has the projector. He is in a wheelchair and his name is Gavin. He only has *Mary Poppins* and *The Poseidon Adventure*, but he prefers *The Poseidon Adventure* so we've seen that seven times. But we tell Mum and Dad that he only shows *Mary Poppins*. In *The Poseidon Adventure*, a tidal wave makes a ocean liner capsize and all the people drown or have to get out through the bottom of the ship in their ball gowns. It is terrifying and I know it makes Leo have nightmares.

"I have been reading in *The Herald*," Mr. F pulls down his World Map that hangs on a roller and points at the Pacific Ocean, "that there's a good possibility of tsunamis being generated from underwater earthquakes anywhere in the Pacific. Maybe off the coast of Chile—*here*. If so, the giant wave would roll right across the ocean, gaining momentum and height as it goes. There is only the Easter Islands — here, between us and Chile. They're nothing. By the time a tsunami hit us—here, on the east coast of New Zealand, the wave could be the height of four two-level houses stacked on top of each other."

Nobody raises a hand. Mr. F slowly drags his pointer from Chile to our island again.

"That's an immense amount of ocean between here and there for it to gain momentum."

It does look 'immense.' At least a foot of blue on the map, that at the top is crammed full of land, in large fancy shapes of countries like Canada, where Mum or Dad go for ages at a time to see their family. At the bottom, where we are, is mainly just blue. New Zealand looks like a sliver. A cut off toenail.

Mr. F rolls another map down, of New Zealand only, and pokes at our island, east of Auckland. "Fifty kilometers of no-hopers," Mum says, and Dad says, "It's a nice place for the kids. It's safe."

"Tryphena is a flat bay. The only sizeable hill is directly behind us, heading northeast. It's not a mountain, but it's a relatively high point of land at this end of the island. So, we're going to imagine we've just heard a tsunami warning on the radio. Pretend we have half an hour to escape the giant wave."

He blows his sports whistle. It shrills inside my head. A chill settles in my chest even though it's hot and flies chase each other outside in the dizzying afternoon heat on the concrete where we all find ourselves a few moments later.

"Okay kids, follow me. Single file."

The whole school troops through the brown wooden gate. We walk, "Don't run!" Mrs. F hisses, along the road that leads up the hill. We are supposed to be in single file, but Leo stubbornly sticks his hand in mine, I can tell he's scared, so I close my fingers over his and we go side by side.

We turn off the road and head up a thin track in the dusty high grass. The top of the hill looms over us. I look down at our house—the shop—where its brown roof shrinks into a small square. The smaller it becomes, the more I worry. What if Mum and Dad are busy with customers and aren't listening to the radio? They're always rushing around with the transistor switched off. The bay is right in front of the house, the waves lap right up to the grass bank when it's full tide. If you look straight out, you can see Channel Rock and after that it's only dark blue. I don't know how many meters it is, but it's enough time to eat a bag of peanuts and drink your box of Just Juice that they give you on the SeaBee that flies from our beach over to Auckland. There's only the flat road between our house and the sea. Will and Matt are studying their correspondence, they're both busy with their thick packages that come with the mail. They won't be listening to the radio. Or watching TV. They will *all* be swallowed by the tsunami.

I want to cry, thinking about the disappearing roof with my parents and big brothers trapped inside, but I am holding Leo's sweaty soft hand. I pretend we have a flashlight shining through our hands.

"Look," I hold my hand up to the sun above the Hauraki Gulf, "can you see the veins? They're blue like the sea."

Leo asks, "Is the su-na-my blue?"

I want to stop and shake him, but he doesn't know the truth behind this drill. The secret that everyone below us will die when they run out of their shops, bachs, and caravans to watch the wave. He can't know or he'll never learn to read, he'll be so afraid of being left with Mrs. F for a mother.

"Yes, the tsunami will be blue like the sea. It's made from sea."

I say this squeezing his chubby hand, crushing his blue veins with mine.

Mrs. F is at the back of the line, with Sebastian. We all hear the scream and instinctively stop and turn. Sebastian lies on the dirt track throwing a tantrum. This is the reason, Mum says, why he shouldn't be in school. He's too young. But Dad points out that Mr. and Mrs. Fuller have to teach all day, so who would take care of Sebastian? Mum says it still isn't right. In fact, it's illegal.

Mrs. F scoops Sebastian up in her fleshy arms, her hair sticks to her neck in the shimmering heat. Sebastian keeps screaming, arching his back, until Mrs. F has to let him down on the track again. She stares at Mr. F. Sebastian rubs his eyes as he howls.

Finally, Mrs. F says, "I'm taking him back down, Jim."

"Alright," Mr. F says. His shoulders sag a little. He gives the rest of us a stern look, "but if there's a real tsunami, going up this hill is the only safe place within reach. So, we'd all have to climb this hill, even if it's hot like this, even if it's raining."

Mrs. F leads Sebastian back down the track. They move a lot faster, going downhill.

Russell sticks his hand up, "Couldn't we get the SeaBee to

fly us over to the mainland? Or escape off the island on the Barge?"

Mr. F snorts, "There wouldn't be room. Or time. We're talking about a wall of water so fast, it travels at eight hundred kilometers an hour."

That sounds too fast to be true, but nobody says anything more. We are all saving energy to get to the top. Leo's hand slips in mine. I look up the line, but Ingrid's walking with her head down. I wish she'd look back, to see how good I'm being, holding Leo's hand the whole way. But she won't.

"Can we see the su-na-my soon?" Leo complains. He's tired and puffed. But I can't stop the line. He has to keep going. I say nothing. I hold his hand tighter because he is making me so mad.

Mr. F reaches the apex and we form a circle around him, slowing to a stop, breathing hard in the bright sun. Ingrid comes over to check Leo is okay after being led by me.

"The su-na-my's coming, Ingy."

"No, it isn't. What did you tell him, Skye? Did you scare him?"

"No! I didn't do anything."

Everyone is standing quietly, so Ingrid takes Leo's hand and pushes me back out of her way.

Mr. F counts up. He ticks our blue names off the roll with his red pen. I can see Fenella wriggling like she needs to pee, but none of us dares put up our hands when Mr. F is ticking off the roll.

"We'll be the first thing hit after Chile," he repeats. "The tsunami will come from South America and there's only

Easter Island in between. That's why this island is called Great Barrier Island. We are the barrier between the Pacific and the rest of New Zealand."

I picture those stone statues we learned about in Social Studies. They'll be watching for the blue tower rising toward them, as we are from our little hill.

Ingrid puts up her hand. I don't want her to say something to make Mr. F frown. I just know she's going to say something bad.

"But Mr. Fuller," Ingrid starts. "Won't the wave only swamp the east coast if Easter Island is east?"

We turn to follow Ingrid's outstretched hand, pointing the other way, away from the tiny brown roof, the school and the bay of Mulberry Grove. She points away, over a few hills, to the line of blue marking the beginning of the Pacific and the eastern edge of the Island. It looks far away. Hardly anybody lives out on the east coast. Will says there are only magic mushrooms and dope fields there. I want to know what's magic about mushrooms, but Will never explains the things he says.

"We're talking about a wall of water. The biggest one this century started at Alaska and hit Hawaii. One hundred and fifty people died," he says stiffly.

Nothing is said about the east coast. Ingrid's words take the fear out of us. The hot fear from the Drill gets smaller and smaller. It cores like an onion. I look back down at our bay. Ingrid's right, it's in flat Hauraki Gulf, not the wild Pacific. Even out towards Channel Rock, there are no whitecaps, just blue, soft blue stretching outwards to the mainland.

Ingrid smiles at me and takes Leo's hand. He shrugs it off. He doesn't need it now we're going downhill.

We clamber down quickly, in light skips, taking the hill in little bounds. Leo holds his hands up to the sky as we jog lightly down.

"See, the lines are all blue, like the su-na-my, Skye," he agrees, "it's gonna be so nice when it comes."

Skye, Ingrid, Leo

I TURNED SEVEN WITHOUT MUM—she went to Canada to see her Mum. I looked for Canada on the World Map Political at school—it was big and pink. She'd been gone for ages. When I was sad that I had to have my birthday without her, Dad said, "Oh, come on, little girl, your mother's only been away three weeks. She'll be back in two." He promised she'd bring back a nice present. I was hoping for a doll.

We all sang Happy Birthday to me and it was a nice time. We watched *Ready to Roll* on TV, ate chocolate cake, and then our big brother and sister and dad tucked us all into bed.

ON SKYE'S SEVENTH BIRTHDAY *I* made the cake. Chocolate inside with chocolate icing and chocolate hail. She got lots of presents. Our oldest sister, Junie, made a doll necklace for her out of clay. Mum phoned from Aunt Alannah's house in Vancouver, Canada and talked to Dad, then Skye, then to Junie and even to our big brother, Will. *I didn't even get to talk to her.* Skye was showing off that Mum was bringing her a doll home from Canada. Mum had left 24 days ago and wouldn't be back for another 16.

Leo was being a pest. He kept running everywhere, all

round the balcony, all through the house. He's always being a pest. I told him to cut it out. I told him to cut it out now. He never listened. He was being a real brat.

Then, Leo fell off the balcony. His head hit the grass, not the concrete step, I know, I saw it. Junie came running out and told me off for nothing. I hadn't done anything. There was no reason for her to spank me like that. Will ran down the stairs and through the shop outside to reach Leo, calling out for Dad. Everyone was calling out for Dad because we couldn't call out for Mum. Dad joined Will and they examined Leo. He wasn't bleeding. I could've told them that, I saw it all happen. Skye wriggled in there, beside Leo, crying non-stop. Dad said, "Stand back." He checked inside Leo's eyes with a torch.

"What's your name?" he asked.

"Leo," said Leo.

"How old are you?"

"Now I'm five."

"Good boy," Dad said, "And how many fingers am I holding up?"

"Three," Leo said.

"Okay. I think you're okay."

Dad lifted Leo up and carried him inside. Will carried in Skye. Everyone stared at me like I'd done something.

Will said, "You're always so rough with him, Ingrid. Why don't you play nice? You're nine, you should know better. He's only little."

"He's a slob and a pain," I said, and started to cry.

Nobody said anything nice to me or came to give me a hug, they were all in the bedroom with Leo, patting his arm, asking how he felt; bringing him his favorite stupid stuffed animals. Nobody said anything nice about my cake when we finally ate it.

Skye asked, "Can we take some cake in for Leo?"

And Dad said, "No, little girl, he's asleep now. I think it's best we don't tell your mother what Ingrid did."

I shouted, "I didn't do anything!" and ran off to cry in the bathroom until finally Dad came in and said, "Of course, you didn't mean it." I sniffed and said nothing. He gave me a big bear hug and we went and watched *The Love Boat* with Junie and Will. Skye had already been sent off to bed because she was still only seven and she can *never, ever* stay up as late as me.

WE ATE SPAGHETTI for Skye's birthday and she got a lot of presents. A doll from Junie and books and a schoolbag and skippy rope and knucklebones. But she put them away in our room and then we played on the balcony with the skippy rope. But Ingrid didn't wanna turn the rope for me cos she said I didn't jump at the right time, so I cried and then she pushed me off.

I saw the ground come up and I hit with no noise. Just the ground and then ssshh. Then the air came back but I still couldn't scream. I just felt bad. All my body was sore and my head. I didn't feel like moving, just lying there. I didn't want to say anything and then Dad came and picked me up and I said, "Where's Mum? I want Mum."

And nobody told me where was Mum, they just put me in Mum and Dad's big bed. It was so big and Dad put me right in the middle with all the pillows and Skye sneaked in and gave me some cake. It was chocolate cake and it was really nice and I wanted some more but I just maybe wanted to go to sleep. And right before I shut my eyes Ingrid came in and said I ruined Skye's birthday and I had to stop being a pain.

Anon 3

I WAS TWELVE when we went to Toronto to our uncle's split-level house in Oakville. There were words that brought us to this: "sale of the house," "falling through," and "mortgage payments." I was in sharing with cousin Rowena, who drank rum and Coke out of a plastic thermos she hid under her bed and sent me every midnight to make her French fries in their deep fryer.

I learned things about Rowena:

She ate nothing all day except the fries.

She was "almost doing it" with her boyfriend Jason, although I wasn't sure if he was a real boyfriend or she was just doing it with him.

She was failing Canadian History, Calculus, English, and Applied Life Studies.

She had seen *Purple Rain* at the multiplex beside the Giant Tiger fifteen times even though she was fifteen and it was R16.

Rowena had to have music to fall asleep, but only one tape: Purple Rain. I couldn't fall asleep with music playing; I waited until the tape ended with its rattling clunk, which amazingly never woke Rowena up. The neon streetlight shone into my eyes because Rowena liked the blinds half shut. There was never so much light and music where we lived before on Prince Edward Island. Toronto was an enormous city I could be lost in, was lost in, would always be lost in.

At first it was only at lunchtime that I'd go out into the city. I went to Ridgeway Elementary School by myself because my sister was in junior high with Rowena over at Algonquin High. Lunchtimes at Ridgeway it was either stay in or go out, with the doors locked at 12.05 until 1.10. I tried to stay indoors. I slunk around the library, taking a long time to eat my baloney sandwich then browsing books, pretending to belong, eventually sitting in a corner with something open I wasn't seeing. There were a lot of others in the library at lunchtime but nobody spoke to me, some were the girls who made fun of my clothes, calling me "hick" or "the Eastie." "Go back East!" they teased. They hated my accent, it wasn't right, too provincial. PEI had red earth, lots of potatoes, *Anne of Green Gables*. These things were despised.

Soon I was drawn outside. The wind was mean, pulling my hair, slapping me. I walked round the block, then round the block plus the next, then round the block plus the next and off on a straight line from the edge of that block into industrial nothing places where nobody lived, no cats sat outside, no dogs barked, there was only me with my hands shoved into the pockets of my hand-me-down ski jacket, nostrils singing from the cold, eyes smarting, the below-freezing air sniping with every blink. The streets snaked into a maze of pale gray concrete sidewalks the color of gone dad's eyes, fire hydrants in accusatory yellow, dead-looking duplexes with cedar cladding, patches of lawn out front currently choked with huge snow banks. Cold, white, nothingness filled my mind. I wiped my nose constantly with Rowena's rejected scarf.

I started not going back for 1.10, which meant I missed Music at 1.15, Geography at 2.00, recess, then Math at 3.15. Or History, Grammar then Science. It slipped easily into every afternoon from Monday to Friday. Now Wednesday didn't mean Wednesday to me, it was a thin layer of jelly over a deep cold bowl of something miserable, impossible to stay upright upon. It was easy to slip past or through that surface "agreed idea" of Wednesday or Thursday or Monday, going instead into an unnamable non-place where there was no bell ringing to change class, no double doors locked to keep you in or out, I was underneath all that—barely able to see up to know where to break back through and rejoin the real world.

I found myself often at the Giant Tiger at the top of Alexander Rise; surprised to see it was already 4.15. A safe time, the time I could feasibly be out of school, standing before the Giant Tiger. I'd go in; not looking at the check-out, not wanting to see which counter Mom worked that day. It was a source of hot red embarrassment that she worked full time at the Giant Tiger while we were in Toronto. I snaked down the aisles to Make-Up and Teen Apparel, passing my hands over the gray marl sweaters and baby pink tracksuits, lifting small items like hair ties, blusher, and nail polish, slipping them deep into my pockets. I walked out slowly every time, not in a rush, not being obvious. Nobody ever stopped me.

Once outside I'd press my head against the wall of windows to see where Mom was, hands busy, smile shy. Her check-out counter changed from 13 to 19 to 5, but she was always there, not seeing me, not knowing what I'd done, was doing, might always be doing. I shoplifted every school day for a month. I hid the things under my side of Rowena's bed.

One night I turned on the oil to heat up, got the bag of frozen McCain's crinkle cut from the chest freezer in the basement, but when I returned I heard a noise in the kitchen. I curled myself around the walls in the lounge, sidling closer. It was cousin Zed.

He leaned up against the counter, still in his duffel jacket. I realized he'd been drinking because when he turned off the oil he fumbled twisting the black dial.

He said, "What are you doing down here?"

I hid the frozen fries behind my back, they sent freezing chills over my body. My nubby-nothing-breasts stood out against my castoff nightgown. Zed took no notice, busy with a bottle of Coke.

"Nothing," I said.

"Who's heating up this oil?"

"Are you drunk?" I asked.

"Gosh, no," he replied. But he didn't sound convinced.

He leaned against the wall for a few long moments, then moved off down to the rec room. I dashed upstairs.

"I can't make the fries, Ro, Zed caught me."

"Don't be a baby. Go make them now. Zed doesn't give a shit."

I went back, started the job over. The oil slowly heated up to 400°F and I wondered what would happen if I put Zed's earmuffs into the wire basket and dropped them in.

I noticed some things changing:

I dreamed rude dreams about Prince, on his motorcycle.

I started trying on Rowena's make-up.

I stopped eating anything except French fries.

A girl called Margo in my home class invited me to celebrate her birthday, which meant going to the mall in the afternoon then eating at Dairy Queen. I had no money to shop or eat, but Margo's dad had given her money for our burgers and sundaes. I was so happy that I had a present for her. I'd wrapped up everything under the bed: seven Kissing Potion lip balms, three Maybelline blushers, eight Gemey mascaras, two eyelash curlers, 112 packets of Chiclets, 22 bobble hair ties, and 12 hair bands. She showed her dad when he came to pick up us, saying I was the kindest person she knew.

Her dad didn't look convinced.

Skye 3

JUNIE'S WEDDING DAY fell on a Tuesday in July, 1983. The oldest in the family but second to marry, Junie did things in the right order, meaning there was no gun in sight.

Her dress was bought off-the-rack in Charlottetown. It was ivory, Grecian, ethereal with pointed lace panels floating over her bronzed forearms and skimming her golden ankles. It pulled in at the waist but fell straight down to midway between calves and heels. She wore a circlet around her head with a translucent lace veil fluttering over her natural mocha brown ringlets. She carried a simple bunch of cream roses, mirroring the marzipan cream roses Mother made to decorate the twenty-pound wedding cake. Her eyes, a Mediterranean turquoise, were cleverly made-up with a silver shimmery eyeshadow and her trademark sapphire blue mascara that Junie did herself, turning down Nadine's offer to help. Junie did make one concession and borrowed a dab of Nadine's stage blush—a fantastic cream blush that needed blending in with your fingertips. And it looked like she'd smeared on Mother's one-and-only lipstick: Revlon ColorStay 55 Coral Dream.

We were all there, but none of the groom's side could be.

There were no friends in attendance. The only outsider was Susan Banks, the Unitarian minister who married them. The minister wore a cream magisterial robe with an accompanying gold and green sash. With her halo of blonde curls she looked more related to Junie than the rest of us with our straight lank locks.

We sat silently in the church, all ignoring the random babbling and shrill outbursts of two year-old, doll-clutching Sienna. I marveled hearing my now brother-in-law's full name read aloud: Oscar Ronald Visser-Bates. It sounded fitting paired up with our sister's full name: June Miranda Adele Ventures. Oscar's name gave off impressions of nobility. He was born in Zimbabwe, fled as a child, we'd met his brother and sister, and the old and terrifying Mrs. Visser-Bates on their farm, but none of them had traveled for this day and we regarded Oscar as an orphan: lost, needing us to welcome him like a tsunami of Ventures, and we did with open arms.

Will, then twenty, and surfing the crest of a wave of adoring females (radio DJing, university parties, and beer fests had made him the most adored guy on campus), pretended in the photos to be the drunk side-kick of Oscar fresh from the Stag Night they never enjoyed, the two of them propping each other up, ties askew, eyes squirreling and squinting in the sunlight, feet tangled, knees bent, in a brotherly photo of 'Welcome to the Family.'

The adults drank cider, the kids got Creaming Soda and Mother's 12lb turkey was demolished with her mashed potatoes, obligatory peas and carrots, and the never-enough-for-us stuffing. Mother's stuffing was just stale bread, onion, garlic, butter, and thyme but we devoured it as if maternal love in there. As if that stuffing was our childhood.

Nadine, freshly single, carting Sienna perpetually on one

hip, wore a sky-blue long crêpe dress and with her new haircut from her sojourn to Florence, Italy, she channeled pure Princess Diana, everyone's new favorite royal. Sienna wore a yellow and white sundress that was dirt-smeared in minutes. Matt kept ducking out of the room to hear updates on the cricket and anyone could see Oscar was itching to go off and listen, too.

We were the flower girls: Ingrid and I, in identical white frilly dresses and carefully combed hair. Ingrid had on white stockings and patent black shoes. But I wore flesh colored stockings with yellow mules. Why didn't I have black shoes? I didn't think I looked good enough. I bowed my head and slouched. Mother did nothing to fix my yellow mules disaster. She said I wasn't the bride and nobody was looking anyway.

Leo wore a blue corduroy suit and said, "Pull my finger," repeatedly, and if someone (i.e. Will) indulged him and pulled his finger he obediently farted and giggled hysterically. Junie overheard and scowled her famous furrowed-forehead scowl that she'd inherited from Father and would be the cause of the first permanent wrinkles on her heart-shaped face.

I'm not sure on this wedding day how Junie feels. She seems to be from a different family, setting herself apart from the rest of us since she was sixteen and left home. She was always far ahead of the rest of us rabble. There are no memories of her playing with us younger kids. No games, silliness, book-reading or outings. One day we found her and Nadine's boxes of Tampax in the oversized cupboard where we'd go to play. We had no idea what they were or their function, so we ripped a few apart to understand them more.

She slid open the door, caught us with a shredded mess of cotton-on-a-string and yelled, "Get out of here right now!" I'm sure to her we were underfoot little devils.

After the moist, heady wedding cake with real rum in it (but cooked, and thus harmless although we didn't understand the difference and somehow felt drunk), we piled into the Ford Pinto station wagon to drive to Ottawa with the newlyweds. Junie and Oscar wouldn't be with us all the way to Ottawa— their destination was Burlington, Vermont, to catch a cheap flight to Europe. Their suitcases took up most of the boot and Ingrid and I had to accordion ourselves around lumpy rock-hard bags, our noses pressed into the backs of the heads in front of us. Will drove, taking turns with Matt. Oscar needed the passenger seat for his long legs and status as new member of the clan, Mother sat in the back urging Will to drive slower, Junie—now out of her bridal finery and in jeans and a white cotton brocaded blouse—sat on one side of Mother with Matt (when not driving) wedged in on the other, his ear glued to his transistor radio with a blow-by-blow account of every pitch, run, and leg-before-wicket.

Any time Ingrid or I complained we were dizzy from the car exhaust fumes or had foot cramps from the sardine conditions Mother hissed, "Pipe down, you two aren't supposed to be on this trip!" It was true, we were to stay back like Leo with Father and Nadine, but last minute either Father had thought better of taking care of all three of us or we didn't want the party to end. We generally fought and screamed to be anywhere Will was going to be. Leo's face was red with tears when we drove away from them.

We wound our way, car bursting with Ventures and now the fresh Visser-Bates couple, through New Brunswick to the American border and into Vermont. They made their plane— just. They made it to London in time for Oscar to go watch the Ashes at Lord's (Cricket was possibly the real impetus to catch that cheap flight, not the lures of Europe). We breathed deeper, stretched our legs, climbed into our rightful seats up in the proper backseat once Junie and Oscar and their belongings were discharged. They spent their wedding night on a chartered flight with 325 other passengers—their bodily gases and bad movie options. Junie took a quarter of her wedding cake with them on their travels. Mother brought another quarter with us to Ottawa to share with Aunt Alannah and the cousins. And Matt hoarded a corner as he loved, above any other food in the world, Mother's fruitcake.

NADINE WAS MARRIED FIRST even though she was the second-born. She jumped the gun, so to speak.

A heady, impetuous child, in Mother's conservative opinion, Nadine was an artist from a young age: creative, sensitive, whimsical, fragile for this world. She dressed us up and wrote us plays to act out. She took photographs of us as babies sitting in a yellow field at the end of our road. She sang to us. She filled in the gaps and smoothed over the rough edges of our slap-dash overpopulated upbringing; somehow it was Nadine who gave us what we craved: hugs and love and demonstrations. But to Mother there was something kind of funny going on with Nadine that didn't make sense. To us, Nadine made perfect sense. She was our sunshine.

Nadine left home to go to Vancouver when she was twenty. This sounds young to most people but I guess in our family twenty was the equivalent of old age since Junie set the bar so high by leaving home for university at sixteen. Destined for drama, Nadine took a one-way ticket and enrolled herself at university to study Acting. Who knows how she found her classes, or life in the relatively colossal city of Vancouver, but after a few months Nadine flew home, with a friend. One day we came home from school and they were both there as if they'd never been anywhere else.

When we met him, he was rocking. Reading a very thick book. One foot rocked the chair, the other ankle sat on his knee so he made a triangle with his legs, and his shorts sat loose in his lap. One leg of his shorts hung so loose you could see dark blonde curly hair crawling up his leg. His hair fell straight into his eyes. When Nadine introduced us, he didn't look up. His foot kept rocking the chair. The other foot jumped around in the air. He turned a page of his big book and sighed. He said nothing to us. Not a word. He kept rocking. His hands were strong and his skin was a honey color like his hair. He was reading *Ulysses*. He read very, very fast. After we watched him read a few pages we went to our room to play and later Nadine came in, sat on the lower bunk, stared at the floor and explained nothing.

"He's not used to lots of kids around."

We had a name now. Simon Jest.

Simon was born on either September 29th or 30th, it wasn't known which because he'd been adopted and then his adopted parents died and he was fostered out—his adopted sister went to live with a grandmother, but Simon wasn't taken in—he was on his own from about the age of ten. We couldn't understand how lonely he was.

He and Nadine got married on Christmas Day, 1980. It was a searing hot day. In New Zealand, everything's the opposite, seasons are upside-down. Christmas is beach, sunshine, fish for dinner, swimming. The Christmas trees' needles fall off within days with the heat. The decorations and cards of snowmen, snow queens and ice-skating bears look wrong and the shops don't sell southern hemisphere equivalents. Nadine and Simon were married at Rangimarie, a hippy commune not belonging to any denomination.

Nadine wore a blue dress with white flowers and left her long, straight blonde hair hang down loose. Simon put on a white linen shirt he'd produced from nowhere and wore his usual ripped jeans and leather sandals. Ingrid and I were the flower girls, wearing coral-and-white dresses Mother had made for us out of material with large hibiscus as the pattern and we clutched bunches of wild daisies and snapdragons. The only photo taken included Mother and Father, Nadine, Junie (before she met Oscar), Will, Ingrid, me, and Leo (Matt was away studying something somewhere) and Simon who crouches down in front of Nadine's stomach, his smile hiding what I didn't realize was in there: Sienna was present at the wedding as a six month-old secret, in other words a strange, soccer-ball hardness under Nadine's blue dress.

Again, the wedding guests were only us Ventures with nobody from the groom's side.

It was a fairy tale wedding in a way. Nadine, chubbier

cheeked than we'd remembered, smiled like a Mona Lisa and Simon ran around the front lawn after, persuading Father to open some sparkling wine, bursting with a pride I didn't understand on the day, being eight years old. Mother made her wedding cake again, oozing candied cherries and sultanas and raisins. The scent of the marzipan layer clung to the furnishings upstairs, since the pocket kitchen was open-plan onto the tiny lounge where we lived. After or before eating— it must have been before as even our relaxed parents drew a line at children swimming with full stomachs—we went swimming.

Simon led the way like the Pied Piper of Hamelin, with Will following closely, Junie and Nadine feigned something important to do elsewhere, and us three little kids chased to keep up. We had on our life jackets so it must have been rough seas that day. Mother would have been watching from the triangular windows upstairs in the lounge, like she did when it was rough and we went swimming. Huge waves pummeled us, every one that bore down on us washed us clean of thought, clean even of terror, alive down to our toes. We flung seaweed at Leo who cried as usual and retaliated with jellyfish that Will helped him heap into a throwable missile.

Nutter appeared, the black and white dog who lived down the road, and Simon was so happy to be married at the age of twenty-one into such a loving, wonderful family as ours that he danced with Nutter—holding her by her front legs and swinging her around in the shallow water with her back legs flying out behind. Nutter howled repeatedly. Out of pleasure or fear we couldn't tell.

Then we went inside and got changed, dried off somewhat and sat down to eat Mother's roast chicken with the stuffing. That day she added half a lemon down the carcass before sewing it up. We all complained it didn't taste right and that was the last time Mother tried any fancy deviations from her recipe. We toasted the newlyweds with sparkling grape juice and real wine for the adults, and even Will was allowed a drink. He was seventeen then and grappling with the high school syllabus by correspondence because where we lived was such a remote—Godless some said—strange island off the coast of a strange remote—Godzone some said—country. We knew our island was beyond just remote. No electricity, no sealed roads. Hippies and no hopers. And us, where did that place us? Were we no hopers then? We weren't hippies. Well, except for Nadine and Simon.

Faye 2

FAYE HAD NO PRESSURE to cook for a ton of kids, plus spouses and grandchildren. There was only her and Richard, and two kids for Christmas lunch, not even Sienna was around this year. Leo was obsessed with that low-carb Atkins diet, so potatoes were off the menu. And Nadine was convinced she was allergic to wheat, so no need for gravy. They could eat roast chicken with roasted carrots, frozen peas and beetroot—with Faye's stuffing for those who deigned to eat bread (Richard and her). She'd attempted a fruit cake without flour in it. The cake hadn't risen and was a minefield of raisins, green and red candied cherries, slivered almonds. Richard could make custard to accompany it. He made a good custard. Daffodil-yellow, sweet and viscose. The cake was in dire need of sunny plastic surgery to mask its defaults.

It was already one o'clock. Nadine was late. No surprise there. Nadine was born late when they lived out west on Vancouver Island. Wet and glum British Columbia. Nadine had straw blonde hair and gray eyes. She had won awards for her paintings, had studied art in Italy, had exhibited, but had held down very few jobs. Hadn't learned how to budget for the utility bills. Or so she'd have food at the end of the month.

A few years ago, Faye saw a program about a strain of measles that caused temporal lobe disturbance—it made a kid religious and prone to hallucinations, personality change, psychiatric disturbance, and memory loss—which pretty much fit the bill with Nadine, who came down with measles when she was five. And look how born-again Christian she was. Nadine was so sick with those measles the doctor put her in hospital for three days. She cried and cried and said she had nightmares all the time. Nightmares about being stuck outside in a snowstorm. Which was kind of an odd dream since Nadine had only ever lived in Nanaimo where it never snowed.

Their neighbor, the Munro boy was just as sick. He recovered fine enough, but when the Munro boy turned sixteen, he started hearing voices, became anti-social and then took his father's hunting gun and killed his entire family. Shot the mother, father, his two sisters, and their beautiful collie. Then he shot himself. They lived up in an architect-designed house on Gossamer Drive that Faye coveted. Just look what happened to the Munros living in that beautiful house, when their son had been sick with the same strain of measles. It made Faye shudder. They could've all been murdered in their sleep by Nadine. It made Faye glad her daughter was only hyper-religious and awfully stubborn.

Faye heard the back door open and knew it was Nadine coming in. Not a moment too soon, the chicken would be dried out like a bone and the usual Ontario snowstorm had begun. Outside was a whiteout.

"Oh, there you are!" Faye called.

Nadine stood inside the door with a man at her side. Faye's heart sank.

"I've invited my friend for Christmas lunch. You don't mind?" Nadine's voice was a challenge. She dared her mother to react, so that she could flounce off and eat Christmas lunch at the church, with the homeless or something. Or not even eat, just go sit in Dunkin' Donuts and drink that gut-rotting coffee. Nadine held her mother's gaze for a long moment. The fellow didn't seem to care. He stood there, happy as Larry, waiting to be shown a seat. A sour, sweaty smell wafted over from him and he was dressed worse than a scarecrow.

"Why should I mind?" Faye said. It was no different to Nadine bringing home stray cats that needed a vet, not a bowl of milk. It was no different to Nadine bringing home a variety of her friends, over the years, who added nothing to the conversation and often moved into their home for awhile and who sat like stupid lugs of flesh—all of them epitomizing the block between Faye and her own child.

"This is Jake. Hey, Leo, happy Christmas. This is Jake."

Leo gave the guy one look and said, "Aw, Jesus, Nadine."

Nadine's eyes welled, "Please don't take the Lord's name in vain, Leo."

"Alright, everybody. Nadine, why don't you hang up your and Jake's coats? Leo, find your father. We've got to eat before this bird dries out completely."

"Mom, Jake's a vegetarian. Do we have anything for him?"

"You've got to be kidding. Can he eat free-range?"

"It's alright," Jake drawled. Faye could see him drooling from the smell of roast chicken. Vegetarian, my foot. "I'll make an exception, it's Christmas," said Jake.

"Wonderful," Faye replied.

Richard and Leo came and sat at the table. Richard noted the lanky, grubby stranger, "Oh, Nadine, I see you've brought a homeless person."

"Jake's not homeless. He lives on Augustus Street." Nadine put another setting on the table. Faye handed her another Christmas cracker without a word. Jake was at a loss until Richard pointed at the seat at the end of the table.

"Don't you want to offer your guest something to drink?" Faye asked. "Richard, why don't you open some of that sparkling wine? I could do with a little glass of that."

"Oh brother," Leo muttered under his breath. He knew his mother's ability to get drunk on a thimble of wine. Nadine danced around the kitchen, helping Faye dish up.

"This looks beautiful, Mom. Really beautiful."

"It's overcooked. But never mind."

"Easy on the carrots there, Mom," Leo called from the table. He used to eat the entire fridge weekly. He was so controlled now; like an alien had taken over his body.

"There'll be nothing on your plate. Trust me."

Richard dispensed sparkling wine into small tumblers for everyone. Leo waved his hand over his glass. He only drank water, unless he went down to the bar to have a few Molson Light with his friends. Jake sat so upright his muscles had practically atrophied. But when his glass was full, he lunged.

"Merry Christmas," he said with fake gusto and downed half of it. Richard finished pouring and placed the bottle near Leo to guard it.

Nadine set down the plates and Faye followed with the rest of the condiments. Faye gave Nadine the seat closest to her pungent friend and sat at the other end, near Leo. She regarded Jake surreptitiously. Yes, he almost looked like someone who'd run amok in nice people's homes and slit their throats with a carving knife for Christmas. He had dark stubble, an undershot jaw, a hunched-over brow obscuring his eyes, and worn-out cuffs on his denim shirt. He didn't wear a belt with his jeans and his feet had been clad in industrial snow boots that Nadine coaxed off him—so he now sat at their table in socks. Faye couldn't see them, but she bet his socks were fused from too few washes.

"Let's eat before it goes stone cold." Faye smoothed her napkin over her lap.

"I'll just say Grace."

Knives and forks paused mid-air as Nadine's head bowed and she launched into a detailed speech to God to thank Him for practically every detail in their world, right down to the cranberry sauce they had the mercy to have on this day and she gave thanks for every other day and most of the details on each of those. Finally, she relented with "Amen."

Jake stopped pretending to bow his head along with her and started scooping meat into his mouth.

The family ate slowly and delicately. Nadine because she hardly ate. Leo because his new way of eating precluded wolfing down a meal. Richard because he cut things up methodically and added dribbles of mustard or cranberry sauce to each forkful. Faye because she'd slaved over the stove to produce the meal. Their uninvited guest, or the cuckoo, as Faye was coming to think of him, scoffed half a breast and a leg before you could say, "Why the hell are you even sitting at our table today?" He slurped his wine—which, granted, was cheap and all fizz with little actual grape, but then again that was probably right up Jake's alley. He made no conversation and kept his head down. All Faye could see of the man was a greasy side-parting clogged with dandruff. She was obliged to bring out the ravaged carcass for seconds. Jake even chewed on the end of the thigh bone, seeking marrow. Nobody spoke much.

Richard made attempts to engage Jake in a little auto-biography, but the man was too engrossed in the stuffing.

"Pour me some more wine, will you, Leo," Faye gestured, ignoring her son's pained look over the tilted bottle.

Nadine chatted—all happy—to her father about the success they'd had in curing one of the flock of her aneurisms and cancer. "Amy's breast cancer has completely gone, Dad. We saw it go. And then the brain tumor just disappeared. We saw that go, too. It floated up right out of the room. It was all from Jesus. Amy is free of pain and everything. It was really beautiful."

"Harrumph," Richard said. His catch-all phrase meaning, *Utter tripe, but I'll go along with it.* "And what happened with your telephone bill in the end? Did they reconnect you?"

The question slid right off Nadine, "And so now that Amy is healed, that's great, isn't it, Dad?"

"It sure is, sweetheart," Richard sighed. "Can you pass me some of that bird, if Jake's left any of it?"

Richard was as blunt as a chainsaw at all times. Faye finished her second glass of the wine and grabbed Leo's hand across the table.

"You're looking just right, now, kiddo. Don't lose any more weight now. You're just perfect. You are eating enough, aren't you?"

"Mom," his tone was brusque as Leo removed his hand. "I'm good. Don't worry about me."

Nadine must've been a bit tipsy. She normally didn't drink either. Leaning against her mother, she laughed, "Leo is so gorgeous now, isn't he? We're so proud of you, Leo. Did you know that? We really love you, Leo, don't we, Mom? And the Lord loves you, too!"

Leo squirmed, along with Faye. They both had an aversion to the 'L' word. They pretended the word 'Lord' grated them. But, 'Love' was just as bad. They watched as Richard and Jake finished off their last forkfuls. As soon as the plates were empty, Leo jumped up and started to clear the table. Jake looked up from the fog of his feeding frenzy. Nadine beamed at him, crinkling up her eyes and forehead in a smile identical to her father's. Richard struck out again into the murky waters of conversation like a man in an oarless boat.

"Augustus Street, eh? Which end would that be?"

"Near the bottle shop," Jake mumbled.

"And what do you do?"

"Dad!" Nadine admonished, as if it were a dirty question. "Jake's on a sickness benefit. He was in Vietnam."

"The Gulf," Jake interjected.

"And since then, he can't *work*. His nerves are shattered." Nadine placed a hand on Jake's. "But we're praying for him all the time, aren't we?"

"Sure are," Jake nodded.

"I see," Richard said and lapsed into silence, his elbows on the table propping up his head, hands cupping his cheeks. His face drooped with the sudden glycolic influx of bubbles and cranberry sauce. Faye and Leo fluffed around in the kitchen. Both reluctant to rejoin the table.

"What about the presents?" Leo asked.

"Yes!" Faye said. "Why don't we all go and open the presents. Then later we can have cake. I made a special one with no wheat, Nadine."

"That's nice, oh, good. And I have presents, too, of course."

From her bag appeared odd-shaped parcels, wrapped in Nadine's silk scarves. She carried them through to put under the tree.

"Nadine, you've used your scarves to wrap them? They're from all your travels! I have plenty of gift wrap. You can't do that." Faye picked up one of them: it was addressed to 'Leo-y' and swathed in a calico silk she'd brought back from New Delhi. The others utilized her scarves from Italy, France, and another from Portugal. Nadine treasured those scarves.

"I don't need them. It's part of the present." Nadine said in that stubborn tone that warned not to argue with her.

"But men don't need scarves." Faye inspected the gifts. A cerulean blue *foulard* encased something for her.

"Don't worry, Mom. It's all in the hands of the Lord Jesus." Nadine nodded and smiled and Faye could just *shake her*.

Leo added a few items under the tree. It looked quite festive now. They all sat down and again Faye chose the seat farthest from the impostor. Leo sat beside the tree, ready to play Santa, as he loved to do.

"Here then," Leo handed Jake his sole present.

Jake did his best to look humble, "You shouldn't have, Nade. After you went and invited me and your parents here have been so hospitable."

Faye felt like saying, *Shut your pie hole and get on with it.* Instead she found herself digging her nails into the palms of her hands. Red crescents formed to distract her from throwing this bum out on his ear. The sparkling wine hadn't been enough of a bolster. She was dog tired, tired of all these Christmases. They never ended up the occasions she hoped for. Leo sat cross-legged, almost like a meditation guru, yet eyeing Jake like he wanted to swing a punch at him. Nadine bit her lip waiting to see if her gift was liked. Richard was focused on a blank space of the wall—God knows why—no doubt some sudden calculus equation required his attention. Faye sighed loudly. Jake heard and got on with opening his fuchsia *sciarpa*.

Inside was a mixing bowl made of teal enamel that Faye herself had given to Nadine for Christmas five years ago.

Faye watched Jake feign thrill at his gift. Faye's eyes burned. She hoped at least that Nadine had *forgotten* the bowl was a gift from her mother. That at least it wasn't on purpose.

Then Richard noticed.

"Hey, that's that bowl your mother gave you... what year was it...?"

"No, it *isn't*, Richard, you're imagining things," Faye said, her voice low and fast. Jake and Nadine stopped their *thank you* and modest *it-was-nothing* charade. Nadine frowned—trying to remember? Or to come up with an argument to justify the regiving of the bowl?

"It was Christmas five years ago. Your mother gave you that very bowl. I gather it was surplus to your kitchen needs?" Richard plowed on.

"She can do anything she likes with her own bowl," Faye retorted. That was all it took, she could've said, *Oh look, a purple pig flying at five hundred feet,* the effect would have been the same.

Nadine stood abruptly, tears flying, and went straight for their coats. Jake twigged when she handed him his snow boots and he stood, too, unsure how to react and staring at Nadine for emotional cues—self-riotous? piqued? crippled with sadness? Nadine didn't touch her presents or look anyone in the eye. She was mad. Jake straightened, cued up to be mad along with her.

"We're going now," Nadine said. "Thanks for being so critical, Mom, again. I can't do anything right, can I? Well, you won't have to worry about me, we're going. Come on, Jake."

Jake had left the bowl in the armchair's lap. Nadine glared until he retrieved it, cradling it in the crook of his arm as if it were their child. Leo watched with no comment—he'd seen it all before. Emotional pyrotechnics at Christmas were an annual given. Richard's oil over troubled waters came too late, "Come on, now, Nadine. There's no need to get all hot under the collar."

They let themselves out into the snowstorm.

Faye sighed, "I'll have to go see her tomorrow with her presents. Why did you have to go and say where the bowl was from? She obviously didn't have any money to buy presents. You're so tactless, Richard."

Leo snorted, "Like your body language wasn't screaming at the guy to get out of your house!"

"Sure, I didn't want that drunken bum hanging around all day, but I didn't want Nadine to go with him."

The telephone rang. Faye looked at Richard.

"You get it. I'm exhausted. I'll talk to whoever afterwards."

Faye curled up on the couch and watched Leo open his presents while Richard hee-hawed with laughter with whoever was on the other end. She thought of Nadine out in the cold, walking back into town (unless that good-for-nothing had a vehicle) walking the mile and a half back into town through the heavy snow. She imagined being inside Nadine's mind and seeing everything as a slight against her. She imagined it as snow swirling around you, where everyone's safe inside but you're locked outside, walking in a snowstorm. Always walking and walking and you can never go inside where it's warm.

Acknowledgments

"Betty" stems from my novel *Polaroid Nights*, which received a grant from Creative New Zealand in 1996. I thank the funding committee for that support based on my first pages. "Betty" is chapter one of *Polaroids: Red Eyed*. "Betty or Alabama" is a prequel before *Red Eyed*.

Many of these stories began in classes, workshops, and writing camps with some inspiring authors, specifically WICE in Paris, the Creative Writing course at the University of Auckland, the Friday night class at the British Institute of Paris, and NaNoWriMo.

Huge thanks to Anna Cowie & Spencer Kebbell at www.thepixelpusher.co.uk for the beautiful cover. Thanks to Vicki at www.velvetmorningpress.com for marketing. Thanks for years of encouragement to: Agnès V, Alex F, Andrew M, Elena K, Fran V-B, Helen M, Jane Grey, Janet SC, Jessica M, Kina Sai, Keely G, Krishna B, Kristin D, Laurel Z, Louise K, Marie H, Maxine B, Nhan C, Nicola F, Nicola K, Shannon M, Shena W, Yann S & Yvonne L. With love to Leanne, Jocelyn, John, Bill, Jacqui & Sam, to Blerina, Stella & Louise, and nieces & nephews.

Love and gratitude to Jennifer Butler for introducing these stories. Her own amazing work is found at www.jamesjennifergeorgina.com. Thanks to Lara Stancich for ace typo-spotting.

Love, adoration and thanks to my darling, Mickaël, and our two little 'gone' girls, Béa and Vivie. *Et un grand merci à mes beaux-parents*, Raymonde & Daniel *qui, grâce aux nombreuses "petites vacances" organisées pour nos filles, m'ont permis de libérer le temps nécessaire à l'écriture et la publication de ce livre.*

Contact the Author

If you enjoyed *Triumph: Collected Stories*, please head over to my website lizziehbooks.com where you can subscribe and receive a free novella: *This is Not a Paris Love Story*, plus be updated on promotions, giveaways and competitions to win goodies.

Please leave a review on Amazon.com – drop me a note (via lizzie@lizziehbooks.com, editordeluxe.com, Facebook page Lizzie Harwood Books, or @lizziehbooks on Twitter) when you've posted your review and I'll send you a Bonus Story about the Island.

If you need a book editor for your own tomes, contact me via editordeluxe.com. Thank you for reading and look out for my memoir, *Xamnesia: Everything I Forgot in my Search for an Unreal Life* and book one of my quirky suspense series, *Polaroids: Red Eyed*.